PROFESSOR SPARROW

And the Clear Creek History Mystery

By Jill Glassco

Deep Sea Publishing, LLC

COPYRIGHT PAGE

TABLE OF CONTENTS

For

My daughter, Rebecca.

Many thanks for allowing me to ENLARGE and *s-t-r-e-t-c-h* your Professor Sparrow story. You are a remarkable young woman, and I love you dearly.

And a very special thank you to my editors: Bruce Aufhammer, Wayne Smith, Ashley Marshall, James Marshall, and Tammy Lovely. Your valuable work embellished and strengthened this history mystery.

CHAPTER 1:
PROFESSOR SPARROW

"And he puts spiders in Halloween candy," whispered nine-year-old Isaac.

"No way," Dustin said.

"Tell him, Jacob."

Moon shadows draped the large, time-worn house. A lonesome "whip-poor-will, whip-poor-will, whip-poor-will" called from the darkness.

Thirteen-year-old Jacob glanced over both shoulders. "Well, Caleb said that Logan said that his big brother said that when he and his friends rang the doorbell last Halloween, the front door cracked open and a crinkly, old hand threw candy at 'em. And when they got home, they found bajillions of spiders crawling out of their bags."

Dustin looked bug-eyed. "Whoa," he croaked.

"And the very next week, Professor Sparrow built this huge, iron fence all the way around his property and put those ginormous gates with padlocks across the driveway."

The wooded yard suddenly lit up like a football field.

"Run!" Dustin yelled.

The boys scrambled over each other like puppies over chicken and dumplings and hightailed it down Rabbit Road. Dogs barked at the pounding feet, and pajama-clad neighbors stepped out to see all the fuss and feathers.

"I dro...I dropped my flashlight," Isaac panted.

Jacob pulled his little brother by the arm. "Forget the flashlight. Come on. Let's get out of here!"

Running tennis shoes crunched dry, September leaves across the bridge and past Clear Creek Cemetery where tall tombstones stood like sentinels over the dismal graves. The boys crashed through the woods, dodging low-hanging branches and tearing through thorny briars. Like a three-man race, the trio burst from the thicket, sped down Mulberry Street, and dove into the Coleman tent in

Jacob and Isaac's backyard. They rolled on the ground, laughing and gasping for air.

"Boys!" a deep voice boomed outside the zip-locked canvas.

Jacob shot upright. "Yeah, Dad?"

"It's getting late. You guys need to get some sleep."

"Okay, Dad."

Isaac covered his mouth to smother a giggle. "Night, Dad," he called.

"Good night, guys."

"Whew! That was close," Jacob whispered. "Isaac, not a word about going to Professor Sparrow's."

"But Dad said…"

"Not one word or I'll never let you camp out with me again."

Isaac sighed. "Okay."

~

Professor Sparrow closed the heavy curtains and switched off the flood lights.

"Kids. Humph," he muttered. "What kind of parents let their children roam the streets this time of night?"

"Meow."

A black and gray tabby wound around the old man's woolen trousers. The professor stooped to scratch the fluffy back. Morton purred like a new Rolls-Royce.

~

Benjamin Harrison Sparrow had joined the history department at Indiana University near Clear Creek in 1978 and moved into the small town's oldest, pre-Civil War mansion. Young Professor Sparrow proved to be an American-history, walking encyclopedia. Nevertheless, both students and faculty found the new instructor aloof and rather strange.

"He's an oddball, all right," Professor Miller said. "I came back to the school late one night to pick up some papers, and there was Sparrow, just standing at the end of the hall. I spoke, but he never uttered a word. It didn't take me fifteen seconds to grab those papers, and when I got back to the hall—POOF—he was gone. Elevator still open on the fifth floor. No footsteps in the stairwell. Like he just vanished into thin air."

~

The aging professor shuffled back to an oversized desk. The old library smelled of leather. Dusty shelves packed with books from floor to ceiling stretched around three walls. He carefully folded a yellowed sheet of paper, buried it at the bottom of a metal box, and locked the lid.

"Our secret, Morton," Professor Sparrow twittered and dropped the key into his coat pocket. "Still our little secret."

"Meow."

REFLECTIONS
POINTS TO PONDER

Gossip is idle talk or rumors. How did Isaac "know" that Professor Sparrow put spiders in Halloween candy?

_____

_____

WHAT DOES GOD SAY?

"A gossip goes around telling secrets, but those who are trustworthy can keep a confidence." (Proverbs 11:13)

"A troublemaker plants seeds of strife; gossip separates the best of friends." (Proverbs 16:28)

"Wrongdoers eagerly listen to gossip; liars pay close attention to slander." (Proverbs 17:4)

"A gossip goes around telling secrets, so don't hang around with chatterers." (Proverbs 20:19)

LIVE WHAT YOU LEARN

What are three ways to safeguard against gossiping?

1.

2.

3.

CHAPTER 2:
NEAR POST

"Can I have more bacon, Mom?" Isaac asked at breakfast the next morning.

"*May* I have more bacon, *please*," Rebekah Fickle corrected her dark-haired, blue-eyed boy and passed the loaded platter to Isaac.

Cheerful sunlight poured through the windowpanes, painting bright squares on the kitchen's white-tile floor. Two colorful parakeets, Squirt and Shiloh, chirped in a tall cage nested in one corner, and Lucy, the Australian shepherd, napped under Jacob's chair. Dustin studied the happy faces around the table. He felt like a guest of the Cleavers from the old sitcom *Leave It to Beaver.*

All Mrs. Fickle needs are June Cleaver's high heels and pearl necklace, Dustin silently scoffed.

Stephen Fickle spread a slab of butter on a hot biscuit. "So, Dustin, tell us about your family," he said. "When did you guys move to Clear Creek?"

And all he needs is Ward's morning edition of the <u>Mayfield Press,</u> Dustin thought but said, "Oh, about a year ago. It's just me and my mom and my little

11

sister…right now. My dad's, uh…my dad's in Washington D.C. He's a really important general at the Pentagon, so I don't see him very much."

"A general? Wow! What branch of service?" Stephen said.

"Branch of service? Oh, uh, na…I mean, ar…army. Yeah, he's an army general," Dustin stammered.

"Cool. Does your mom work outside the home?"

"Yeah, she's a realtor."

"What's a realtor?" Isaac asked.

"Someone that sells houses," Rebekah explained.

"Have you guys found a church home since you moved to Clear Creek?" Stephen said.

"Nah, my mom works a lot. She likes to sleep in on Sundays."

"Well, if you and your sister would like to go to church sometime, you're welcome to go with us," Rebekah said.

"Thanks, but I do my homework on Sundays."

Jacob snickered. *Homework? Yeah right. You never do your homework,* he thought.

"Dad is the children's director at our church," Elizabeth, Jacob and Isaac's eleven-year-old sister, said. "It's really fun. You should come."

After breakfast, Rebekah threw the leftovers in the fridge and stacked the dirty dishes in the sink. "Hurry up, guys," she said. "It's almost time for the soccer game. Do you have your cleats?"

Jacob and Dustin both nodded.

"Water bottles?"

"Mine's in the tent. I'll run get it," Dustin said and trotted down the stairs.

Jacob started after his friend, but a firm hand on the shoulder stopped him.

"Son, we need to talk after dinner tonight," Stephen said.

"Yes, sir."

Jacob shot an accusing look toward Isaac. His little brother fiercely shook his head and mouthed, "I didn't say anything. Promise!"

Jacob's heart dropped. *I knew we shouldn't have gone last night.*

The autumn air felt crisp at the middle school soccer field. Dustin and Jacob piled out of the van and joined the red and white team warming up by the south goal. Isaac and Elizabeth scampered to the playground, and Stephen and Rebekah, arms loaded with folding chairs and blankets, hurried to their favorite spot along the sidelines.

Three minutes into the first half, the Nashville Knights scored, but the Clear Creek Cougars answered quickly with a powerful boot from twenty yards out. The score remained tied one to one well into the second half.

With five minutes left on the clock, Tripp, the Cougar's goalkeeper, stopped a Knight's shot and punted it past midfield.

"Way to go, Tripp!" Stephen yelled and clapped.

"Come on, Cougars!" Rebekah shouted.

The Knight's sweeper trapped the ball and passed to his center midfielder. The midfield-man received it and dribbled down field. Dustin, a Cougar midfielder, attacked, but the Knight passed to his striker. The striker dropped the ball back to the left fullback. He kicked a long pass to the outside midfielder on the far sideline. The Knight's midfielder crossed it back to his left forward. Jacob, the Cougar's right fullback, attacked. Both players landed on the ground, and the ball sailed into no man's land.

Three minutes on the clock.

A Knight striker moved quickly to the ball and booted it to the right forward. The right forward took a shot. In a full stretch, Tripp saved the goal with a catch and threw the ball overhead to his left fullback. The fullback kicked down field to the left striker, but a Knight stole the ball and, on a fast break, dribbled down the near sideline. Jacob attacked again, stole the ball, and passed to Dustin at midfield. Dustin streaked down the near sideline and passed to Caleb. The Knight's goalkeeper ran forward and tackled Caleb. The ball landed five yards in front of Jacob. As quick as lightning, Jacob was on the ball, pushed it up field in full stride, and took a long shot. The Knight's goalkeeper jumped. He tipped the ball over the goal and out of bounds.

"Take the corner kick, Jacob!" Coach Tom shouted.

Nine seconds on the clock.

Jacob lined up. BOOM! The ball flew to Dustin at far post. He headed it toward the goal. The ball bounced off the post. Jacob charged in and shot with his left foot to near post...

SCORE!!

The whistle blew.

Game over.

Clear Creek Cougars 2, Nashville Knights 1.

REFLECTIONS

POINTS TO PONDER

Lying is speaking an untrue statement with the intent to deceive. Do you think Dustin told the truth about his dad? YES NO

WHAT DOES GOD SAY?

"Keep your tongue from speaking evil and your lips from telling lies!" (Psalm 34:13)

"There are six things the LORD hates—no seven He detests: haughty eyes, a lying tongue, hands that kill the innocent, a heart that plots evil, feet that race to do wrong, a false witness who pours out lies, a person who sows discord in a family." (Proverbs 6:16-19)

"Truthful words stand the test of time but lies are soon exposed. (Proverbs 12:19)

"...[The devil] has always hated the truth, because there is no truth in him. When he lies, it is consistent with his character; for he is a liar and the father of lies." (John 8:44)

LIVE WHAT YOU LEARN

A half-truth is a lie. At home, at school, and everywhere, intentionally speak the truth, the whole truth, and nothing but the truth, so help you God.

CHAPTER 3:
CHOICES

At supper, picky-eater Jacob asked for two more helpings of red beans and rice, delaying as l-o-o-o-o-n-g as possible the inescapable "talk" with his dad. He shoveled spoonful after spoonful into his mouth and slo-o-o-wly chewed.

And chewed.

And chewed.

"My, Jacob, all that running must have made you hungry," his mother teased.

Stephen winked at Rebekah. "Okay, Bud, you've had enough grub to stuff an elephant. You ready to talk now?"

Jacob gulped. "Uh, okay."

Stephen suggested they go outdoors and shoot some hoops. Silently, he prayed for wisdom as he followed Jacob out the front door. Outside, a steel-framed basketball goal—a gift from the kids' grandparents—stood beside the concrete driveway. Stephen dribbled the ball and took a shot.

"So, tell me about last night," he said.

Jacob snatched the rebound and made a one-handed lay-up. Silently, he prayed for mercy.

"Uh, it was fun," Jacob said.

"So, what'd you guys do?"

"Well, we played Spikeball until it got too dark, and then we played steal the flag."

"Cool. Where did you guys *go*?"

"Go?" Jacob squeaked.

"Yeah, where had you been when you came flying across the yard like a cannonball and sailed into the tent? Your mom and I were sitting on the balcony watching," Stephen said.

"Oh," Jacob muttered. He dribbled the leather b-ball back and forth, back and forth between hands. *Here we go,* he thought. "Well…uh…Dustin…had, uh, Dustin had heard about Professor Sparrow, and he, uh, just wanted to see his house."

~

Jacob Fickle was known for his compliant, wired-to-follow-the-rules personality, even as a thirteen-year-old. Blatant disobedience the night before had been out of character and now weighed heavily on his guilty conscience. *Why did I ever let Dustin talk me into going?* he wondered.

~

"Come on, Jacob. You a scaredy-cat?" Dustin had pressured.

"No, but my dad said…"

"We won't be gone long. Besides, *daddy* will never know."

"I…I don't think it's a good idea," Jacob said.

"Chicken!" Dustin taunted.

"Okay, but just over there and right back. Got it? Isaac, you stay here."

"No way," Isaac said. "If you're going, I'm going."

~

Stephen stole the ball and dribbled to the outside. "So, you and Dustin and Isaac went to Professor Sparrow's house?" his dad said.

Disobedience plus dragging the kid brother along. I'm sunk, Jacob thought.

"Yes, sir," Jacob mumbled.

"And you went there because Dustin wanted to go?"

"Yes, sir."

"Jacob, what did I tell you boys before you set up the tent?"

"Not to leave the yard without your permission."

Stephen passed Jacob the ball. "Yep, that's right. So, by choosing to go, you chose to please a friend over obeying me."

Jacob shot. The ball stripped the net. "Yes, sir."

"Nice shot," Stephen said and snagged the rebound. "So, how has your decision affected your relationship with your mom and me?"

"It...uh...made you mad at me?"

Stephen shook his head and arched the ball toward the hoop. "No, we aren't *mad* at you, but your decision has hurt our *trust in* you. So, what are some ways you can rebuild our trust, Jacob?"

Jacob answered carefully, "Maybe...uh, show you that I'll obey the next time?"

"And the next time, and the next, and the time after that," his dad said. "It takes time to rebuild trust, Jacob—time plus responsible behavior."

"Yes, sir."

"Did your choice affect only you?"

"No, sir."

"Who else was influenced?"

"Isaac."

"Yes," Stephen said, "and who else?"

"Dustin."

"What did your behavior say to Isaac and Dustin?"

"That it's okay to disobey if you don't get caught?"

"And what do you need to do about that?"

"Apologize," Jacob said.

"To whom?"

"To Dustin and Isaac."

"Who else?"

"To you and Mom? I'm sorry, Dad."

"Are you sorry you disobeyed or are you sorry you got caught?" Stephen said.

Jacob grinned. "Both."

"Son, you're thirteen years old now and only at the beginning of a long season of having to choose between obedience to us or popularity with your friends. Your mom and I pray that you'll make wise decisions no matter where you are or who you're with and that you'll choose friends that help you make those good decisions."

"Yes, sir."

"What does Coach Tom tell you guys?"

Jacob said, "Show me your friends, and I'll show you your future."

"You need to remember that good advice when you're choosing your close friends."

"Yes, sir."

"And what *always* follows decisions—good or bad?" Stephen asked.

"Consequences."

"That's right. So, because you chose disobedience, no more camping out until you've earned back our trust, *and* you're grounded from friends for the next two weeks."

"But, Dad, Caleb's birthday party's next Saturday," Jacob moaned.

"Sorry, Bud. Missing that party is a consequence of *your* decision and *your* actions. These terms may seem severe, but your decision could have put you, Isaac, and Dustin in danger."

"Yes, sir. But what about Isaac? He disobeyed, too."

"Don't worry about Isaac. You just focus on your own decisions and think about the influence they have on your little brother. He looks up to you, Jacob."

"Yes, sir."

"Now, go tell Isaac I want to talk to him."

Jacob passed the ball to his dad. "Yes, sir," he said and trotted into the house to find his brother.

REFLECTIONS
POINTS TO PONDER

Stephen said that Jacob was at the beginning of a long season of having to choose between popularity with friends and _____ to his parents.

WHAT DOES GOD SAY

"Children, obey your parents because you belong to the LORD, for this is the right thing to do." (Ephesians 6:1)

"Don't be fooled...bad company corrupts good character." (1 Corinthians 15:33)

"Run from anything that stimulates youthful lusts. Instead, pursue righteous living, faithfulness, love, and peace. Enjoy the companionship of those who call on the Lord with pure hearts. (2 Timothy 2:22)

LIVE WHAT YOU LEARN

Coach Tom said, "Show me your friends and I'll show you your future." What does that mean to you?

_____

_____ Think about your close friends. Does your future look good or bad?

_____

25

CHAPTER 4:
THE RIDDLE

"Class, the purpose of this research paper," Mrs. Culpepper, Jacob's seventh grade English teacher, said, "is not only to help you cultivate good writing skills, but also to help you gain a deeper understanding of your community and its roots."

Oh, great, thought Jacob, *two weeks of house arrest finally end and now I'm grounded by homework.*

"You must use at least three reputable sources in developing your paper, and one of the three must include an interview with someone who has lived in Clear Creek at least twenty-five years."

"Twenty-five years!" Caleb whispered to Jacob.

Angela McCartney raised her hand. "Mrs. Culpepper?"

"Yes, Angela."

"Is it okay to interview a family member?"

"Sure, but it could also be someone you've never even met before. However, if that's the case, be safe and take an adult with you. The subject of your research paper is due one week from this Friday. That gives you almost two weeks to get those imaginations churning and come up with your fantastic ideas."

Jacob jotted down the detailed requirements:

- Seven to ten notecards
- Three-page minimum, double-spaced
- 12-point font, New Times Roman, black ink
- Due Friday, November 16th, before Thanksgiving break

"This is gonna be hard," he whispered to Caleb.

"To tell you the truth," Mrs. Culpepper admitted, "when I was your age, I hated research papers, too. But this assignment doesn't have to be a pain in the derriere."

The students giggled.

"What's dairy air?" Caleb whispered.

Jacob snorted.

Mrs. Culpepper cut her eyes toward the boys but never missed a beat encouraging her students to be creative and have fun. "Attitude determines experience," she said, "and a *good* attitude will make all the difference between miserable and enjoyable. Write about your community from the perspective of your own interests. If you like sports, research Clear Creek's athletic history. If it's music or dancing or art or biking or whatever floats your boat, uncover that topic's secrets from the past and

27

take advantage of the wealth of information sitting right at our backdoor at Indiana University."

~

Blocks away on the fifth floor of IU's history building, Professor Sparrow lectured in his characteristically dry voice about the critical role Indiana played in the American Civil War.

"Indiana supplied manpower for the Union as well as funding for much needed equipment and supplies. Indiana's rich farmland produced abundant grain and livestock, which helped feed Northern troops, and its favorable geographic location afforded access to the Ohio River and Great Lakes by means of a progressive railroad network. However, Indiana experienced severe political discord during the war. When the legislature failed to pass a budget, Governor Oliver Morton, in an effort to keep the state government operating, moved outside constitutional authority and secured funding through loans to prevent financial disaster."

"Furthermore, after the war, five Indiana politicians were major party nominees for vice president, and in 1888, one of Indiana's Civil War generals was elected the 23rd president of the United States. It is *your* responsibility, students, to find the names of those five vice-presidential nominees as well as the name and accomplishments of the 23rd U.S. president."

The professor glimpsed the wall clock. "Friday's examination will cover 1800s pre-Civil War up to the Reconstruction period. Class dismissed," he said.

A moan echoed across the theater-style auditorium. Students gathered books and exited the classroom. A tall, athletic-looking young man approached Professor Sparrow who was shuffling a stack of notes on the podium.

"Professor Sparrow," the student said.

The professor never looked up. "Yes, Mr. Williams?"

The old man's shaggy, white hair and bushy mustache reminded Mark Williams of Albert Einstein.

"May I speak with you, sir?" Mark asked.

"Proceed."

"Uh, I didn't do very well on the last two exams, and I have to maintain a 3.0 GPA this semester to keep my scholarship. So, I was wondering if I…if you would allow me to do extra-credit work to raise my grade?"

"Mr. Williams, may I suggest that you use the time you have between now and Friday to adequately prepare for this week's examination," the professor said.

Mark's shoulders drooped. "Yes, sir."

"Also, see me after class on Friday for an extra-credit assignment, and I assure you, Mr. Williams, it will not be a piece of cake."

"Yes, sir! Thank you, Professor Sparrow."

Professor Sparrow returned to his papers.

~

On Friday, Mark was last in line to hand the completed exam to Professor Sparrow. The professor in turn held out an envelope.

"What's this?" Mark asked.

"Your extra-credit assignment," he answered with a sly grin.

"Thanks, Professor Sparrow." Mark opened the envelope and read:

"From times gone by

A mystery lies,

A secret to unveil.

Be swift, my soul,

Be brave and bold

To comfort her travail.

Be jubilant feet

To run and seek,

The story never told.

The truth that hides

From modern eyes

Of ones so brave and bold."

Mark stared blankly at the piece of paper in his hand. "I don't understand, sir."

"Solve the riddle, Mr. Williams—which no one has in forty years—and you'll earn yourself an A+ in American History 101."

"Uh, okay. Thanks, Professor Sparrow," Mark said.

The professor's steel-gray eyes followed Mark Williams out the door. Amusement tugged at the corners of his mouth. *The perfect puzzle*, he silently mused. *A champion conundrum. Will the answer to the riddle and my undreamed-of discovery follow me to the grave? Time will tell— only Father Time will tell.*

The old man laughed aloud.

REFLECTIONS

POINTS TO PONDER

How do you think Mark felt when he didn't understand Prof. Sparrow's riddle? _____

_____

WHAT GOD DOES SAY?

"If you need wisdom, ask our generous God, and He will give it to you. He will not rebuke you for asking." (James 1:5)

"Ask Me and I will tell you remarkable things you do not know about things to come." (Jeremiah 33:3)

"Keep on asking, and you will receive what you ask for. Keep on seeking, and you will find. Keep on knocking, and the door will be opened for you. For everyone who asks, receives. Everyone who seeks, finds. And to everyone who knocks, the door will be opened." (Matthew 7:7-8)

LIVE WHAT YOU LEARN

Do you need wisdom and insight about something?

YES   NO

Ask God now!

CHAPTER 5:
CORE GROUP

Mark snapped the helmet strap and jumped on his silver Schwinn 14-speed.

"Hey, Mark, how do you think you did on the test?" Jonathan, a cross-country teammate, called.

"Better than the last one, hopefully."

"Wanna grab a bite at the cafeteria?" Jonathan said.

"Sorry, man. I've got a meeting at church, and I'm running late."

Mark cut across campus and pedaled full speed down Sycamore Lane onto Rabbit Road. He turned left on Church Street and whipped into the parking lot of Hebron Community Church. A kaleidoscope of stained-glass windows bejeweled the simple, stone sanctuary, and a matching bell tower topped with a white cross hugged its left side. He slipped through double doors and hurried through the vestibule and down the steps to the basement. Ten cackling, punching, running, seventh-grade boys swarmed Fellowship Hall.

"Hey, guys," Mark shouted above the happy pandemonium. "Sorry I'm late. Grab a chair and round up."

Chairs banged across the concrete floor, and a circle formed around Mark, the core-group leader.

"Okay, guys, settle down. Jacob, will you say our opening prayer, please?"

"Sure." Jacob prayed, "Dear Lord, thank You for this day, and thank You for this group. Thank You for Mark and please help him as he teaches us today, and please help us live what we learn. In Jesus' name, Amen."

"Thanks, Jacob. Okay, guys who read King Jehoshaphat's story in 2 Chronicles chapter 20 this week?" Mark asked.

Jacob's hand and three others raised.

"Good job, guys. Help me tell the story to the other guys. And by the way other guys, thanks for your honesty. In this story, was Jehoshaphat having a good day or a bad day?"

"A really bad day," Caleb said.

"Why was it a really bad day, Caleb?"

"'Cause not just one, but three armies were attacking Judah." Caleb answered.

"How did the king feel?"

"Scared," Noah said.

"What did he do?" Mark said.

"He prayed and called everyone in his kingdom—even the kids—to pray too," Elijah said.

"That's right, Elijah," Mark said. "And in his prayer, Jehoshaphat asked God some important questions like: 'O Lord, aren't you the all-powerful God who drove out our enemies before? And won't you do it again?' And, I love this part, the king acknowledged that they were powerless against the mighty armies marching against them, and they didn't know what to do, but their eyes were glued on the Lord. How did God answer Jehoshaphat?"

"Through a prophet," Jacob said.

"What did God tell the prophet to say?"

"He said, 'Don't be afraid. God will fight for you,'" Jacob answered.

Mark nodded. "And as Jehoshaphat commanded Judah's army the next morning, who did he place on the frontlines?"

"Singers," Jacob said.

"And what happened when the choir sang praises to the Lord?"

"All three armies destroyed each other," Caleb said, "and Judah marched in and picked up the thunder."

Mark laughed. "I think you mean *plunder*—that means they gathered all the weapons, clothes, and other valuables. So, guys, what can we learn from Jehoshaphat?"

"When we're scared, we need to pray?" Charlie said.

"Absolutely, Charlie. What else?"

"To ask God what to do when we don't know," Logan said.

"For sure! As you know, our motto is 'live what we learn.' So, how can we live what we've learned today?"

Jacob raised his hand.

"Yes, Jacob?"

"Well, on Monday, Mrs. Culpepper gave us a really hard research paper to do, and I have no idea what to write about."

"Have you prayed about it?"

"No, but I will tonight."

"Good, Jacob. What else guys? What's coming against you?"

"My mom's a single mom," Charlie said, "and works two jobs. It's really hard for her to pay the bills sometimes. I need to pray for her more and encourage her not to be afraid."

"That's awesome, Charlie."

"Mark, what about you?" Charlie asked. "Anything coming against you?"

Mark wagged his head. "Thanks so much for asking, Charlie. As a matter of fact, I'm really struggling to pass American History this semester, and Professor Sparrow gave me an assignment that, like Jacob, I have no idea what to do. I don't even understand what he's talking about."

"What's the assignment?" Jacob said.

Mark pulled the rhyme from his pocket. "I have to solve this riddle. Wanna hear it?"

"Sure," the boys chimed.

"Okay. So, it goes like this:

From times gone by
A mystery lies,
A secret to unveil.

Be swift, my soul,

Be brave and bold

To comfort her travail.

Be jubilant feet

To run and seek,

The story never told.

The truth that hides

From modern eyes

Of ones so brave and bold."

"Wow!" Caleb said. "It's like a real mystery."

"Maybe we can help," Jacob said.

"Yeah!" the others agreed.

"For real? That would be awesome. Thanks, guys," Mark said. "I'll text you the riddle. On second thought, open your notebooks and write it down the old-fashioned way. After that, who's up for a game of human battleship?"

REFLECTIONS
POINTS TO PONDER

What's coming against you today? _____

_____

WHAT GOD DOES GOD SAY?

_____ *(your name), "...Do not be afraid! Don't be discouraged...for the battle is not yours, but God's." (2 Chronicles 20:15)*

_____ *(your name), "Don't be afraid, for I am with you. Don't be discouraged, for I am your God. I will strengthen you and help you. I will hold you up with My victorious right hand!" (Isaiah 41:10)*

"For God has not given you a spirit of fear and timidity, but of power, love, and self-discipline." (2 Timothy 1:7)

LIVE WHAT YOU LEARN

Three powerful weapons to defeat fear:

1. PRAY, in other words, talk to God.

2. SPEAK God's WORD out loud. (I highly recommend Psalm 91.)

3. PRAISE God for who He is and thank Him for all He has done and will do.

CHAPTER 6:
FATHER KNOWS BEST

"And we're gonna help Mark solve the mystery," Jacob said at the dinner table that evening.

Rebekah's face brightened like a Sunday-morning sunrise. "Ooo, like *The Hardy Boys* or *Nancy Drew*. I love a good mystery!"

"Who?" Elizabeth asked.

Her mom laughed. "The Hardy boys and Nancy Drew were characters in mystery novels that your dad and I read when we were kids. My favorite was Nancy Drew's *The Secret of the Old Clock.* That'll be such fun, Jacob. I'll help, too!"

"Thanks," Jacob said. "May I have another roll?"

"Sure," Stephen said. He passed a basket of piping-hot yeast rolls across the table. "And Professor Sparrow said that no one has been able to solve this riddle in forty years?"

"That's what Mark said," Jacob answered.

Following their mealtime tradition, the family chatted about the best and worst parts of their day. Each shared something learned, something funny, something they would change about the day if they could, and any opportunities they'd had to show kindness.

"Hey! I just had an idea, Jacob." Stephen said enthusiastically. "Why don't you write your research paper on Mark's riddle and interview Professor Sparrow?"

Jacob's eyes got as big as a barn owl. "No way. That old man gives me the creeps. Besides, Mrs. Culpepper said to research something *I'm* interested in. So, I was thinking about IU's soccer team."

"You know most of the guys in your class will probably pick a sports topic, but the history mystery would be really unique. And besides, it's an opportunity for you to show Mark kindness by putting his concerns before your own. It's *your* choice, Bud, but I encourage you to ask God," Stephen said.

"That's what Mark said, too—to pray about it. I will, Dad," Jacob promised.

"We should invite Mark to dinner sometime," Rebekah suggested. "I remember how much I missed my family and home cooking when I was away at school."

"That's a great idea," Stephen agreed. "How about next Friday after core group?"

At bedtime, Jacob sat cross-legged on the top bunk in the bedroom he shared with Isaac. The study Bible that Papaw and Mamaw Willowkins had given him last Christmas lay open across his knees. *Jacob Fickle* in silver letters imprinted the black, bonded-leather cover and thumbnail index finders dented the matching silver-edged pages.

Dear Lord, he silently prayed, *thank You for this day and all that You've done for us. Please help Mark solve the riddle and get a good grade in history, and please tell me what to write about. I don't know how in the world You can tell me, but my eyes are on You. In Jesus' name I pray, Amen.*

He flipped to the Biblical Cyclopedic Index in the front and looked up *advice*. There, he found *Kinds of Advice: helpful, rejected, timely, good, and God-inspired.*

"God-inspired advice: see 2 Samuel 17:6-14. That sounds good," he said.

"Be quiet, Jacob," Isaac whined. "I'm trying to go to sleep."

"Sorry," Jacob mumbled.

Well, that didn't help, Jacob thought after reading a story about the Lord thwarting the good counsel of Ahithophel to bring calamity upon Absalom. Next, he turned to "helpful advice" in Exodus 18:12-25 and read: *"This is not good!" Moses' father-in-law exclaimed. "You're going to wear yourself out. This job is too heavy a burden for you to handle all by yourself. Now listen to me, and let me give you a word of advice, and may God be with you. Select from all the people some capable, honest men who fear God to help you."*

Jacob read the passage a second time. Mark's plea spun in his mind: "I'm really struggling...I don't know what to do...Live what you've learned, guys."

Lord, are you telling me to do like Dad said? To help Mark and write my paper on the history mystery?

He remembered Philippians 2:3, a memory verse from core group: *Don't be selfish; don't try to impress others. Be humble, thinking of others as better than yourselves.* Jacob jumped from the top bunk and ran into the hallway.

"Dad!" he hollered.

"Jacob, be quiet!" Isaac yelled and crammed a pillow over his head.

"Yeah, Bud?" Stephen called.

"I'm gonna do it!"

"Do what?"

"Write my paper on the history mystery!"

"Cool!"

"And can I move downstairs to the guest room?"

"Why, Bud?"

"Now that I'm thirteen, don't you think I'm too old to share a room with Isaac? (pause) And besides, I could study the Bible *so* much better down there."

His parents laughed. "Good try, Bud. We'll think about it. Good night."

REFLECTIONS

POINTS TO PONDER

Stephen encouraged Jacob to put Mark's concerns before his own. Describe an opportunity you've had to put others before yourself. _____

_____

WHAT DOES GOD SAY?

"Do to others whatever you would like them to do to you. This is the essence of all that is taught in the law and the prophets." (Matthew 7:12)

"Don't be selfish; don't try to impress others. Be humble, thinking of others as better than yourselves." (Philippians 2:3)

"Jesus replied, 'You must love the LORD your God with all your heart, all your soul, and all your mind.' This is the first and greatest commandment. A second is equally important: 'Love your neighbor as yourself.'" (Matthew 22:37-39)

LIVE WHAT YOU LEARN

Name ways you can put your mom or dad or sister or brother or friend before yourself.

_____

_____

_____

CHAPTER 7:
CLUELESS

Monday morning, Jacob quickly wove in and out of the boys and girls in the crowded seventh-grade hallway. He wanted to be the first one to turn in the research topic to Mrs. Culpepper.

Clear Creek Middle School resembled a Roman numeral three. The administration offices and library stretched across the front—the top bar. A gymnasium and cafeteria lined the rear—the bottom bar, and three buildings stood in-between, one for sixth graders, one for seventh graders, and one for eighth graders—the vertical bars.

Jacob found the English teacher busy at her desk. "Hi, Mrs. Culpepper. Here," he said and handed her a 3 x 5 index card.

Lisa Culpepper lifted her eyes from a mountain of vocabulary tests with a look of surprise. "Is this your paper topic already, Jacob? It's not due till Friday."

"Yes, ma'am. I know," he answered, grinning from ear to ear.

"Clear Creek history mystery," she read aloud. "Interesting. So, what's this mystery about?"

"I don't know yet."

"So...how do you know there is a Clear Creek mystery?" she probed.

"Well, I guess I'm not sure it is a *Clear Creek* history mystery. But Professor Sparrow at the university says there's a history riddle that hasn't been solved in forty years, and he lives in Clear Creek. So, in a way, it's a Clear Creek history mystery," Jacob explained. "Wanna see the riddle?"

"Absolutely."

Jacob pulled the crumpled paper from his pocket and gave it to the teacher. She scanned the lines. "I love it!" she said. "And I can't wait to read your paper."

"Thanks," Jacob said.

"Now, you do understand, Jacob, that if you get into this mystery and discover it's not about Clear Creek, you'll have to start over. Are you willing to take that risk?"

Jacob didn't hesitate a nanosecond. "Yes, ma'am. I think it's worth the risk."

"Good for you. I really hope it works out well."

~

On Friday, Mark showed up to core group dressed as a zany, Roman soldier. An old football helmet, a camo-hunting vest, worn-out cleats, a dented garbage can lid, and a plastic, Star-Wars lightsaber served as his "Armor of God" as described in Ephesians chapter six. After the lively, animated lesson, he and Jacob pedaled toward Mulberry Street.

Jacob said, "Today's lesson was awesome, Mark."

"Glad you liked it," Mark said. "My dad taught me the Armor of God when I was a little kid. We had to pray on the armor *every* morning before school."

Jacob laughed. "That's funny."

"We loved it. He'd line us up and make us stand at attention. And then he'd yell like a drill sergeant: 'Kids, stand strong in the Lord and the power of His might! Gird your loins with TRUTH.' We'd bellow, 'Yes, sir!' and then buckle our imaginary belts."

"My mom said my granddaddy used to make them do the same thing."

"You're kidding!" Mark said. "'Put on the breastplate of RIGHTEOUSNESS,' he'd roar. 'Shod your feet with the Gospel of PEACE. Lift high that shield of FAITH. Cover your mind with the helmet of SALVATION, and raise the Sword of the Spirit, which is the WORD of God, PRAYING at all times.' We'd yell, 'Yes, sir!' and then throw on our backpacks and run to the bus stop."

Jacob and Mark dropped their bikes in the spacious backyard and burst inside through the basement door. "Mom, we're home!" Jacob shouted.

Rebekah finished stirring a steaming pot of beans on the stove and then checked the biscuits in the oven. "Great," she said. "Come on up. Dinner's almost ready. Y'all hungry?"

"Starving!" Mark answered as they tromped up the steps. "Thanks for inviting me over, Mrs. Fickle. Something smells *so* good! I'm getting awfully tired of Ramen Noodles."

Stephen laughed. "I remember those days. Ramen Noodles and peanut butter and jelly sandwiches—the staple foods of college students."

"Well, tonight you're feasting on chicken and rice casserole, green beans, copper-penny carrots, and angel biscuits," Rebekah said.

At the supper table, the family and Mark joined hands while Stephen thanked God for the delicious food and the Lord's many blessings. Pleasant conversation after the prayer revealed that Mark had grown up in Spencer, a small town in middle Tennessee, and had come to IU on a cross-country scholarship.

"You must be really good to get a scholarship," Stephen said.

"He was Tennessee's cross-country state champion his senior year," Jacob bragged.

"That's awesome, Mark," Rebekah said. "Years ago, Stephen and I were visiting Stephen's grandmother in Cookeville, and we actually passed through your hometown on our way to Fall Creek Falls State Park. Beautiful country."

Mark's face lit up. "For real? I worked at that park every summer all through high school."

"What a great summer job—working outdoors in God's magnificent creation," Stephen said. "And, Mark, we really appreciate your working with the boys this fall in core group. Jacob tells us that you know a lot about the Bible."

"Oh, I love core group. The guys are great and a lot of fun to hang out with," Mark said. "My dad's a pastor, so I've been in church all my life. God's word has always been important to my family and me."

"Do you have any brothers and sisters?" Isaac said.

"I sure do, Isaac. I have a sister named Anna Grace and three brothers—Matthew, Luke, and John."

Stephen grinned. "And you're Mark. You must be a *full gospel* family,"

Mark cackled. Jacob's cheeks burned beet red. "A daddy joke," he mumbled apologetically.

"Mark, I'm so intrigued with Professor Sparrow's mysterious riddle. Have you made any progress in solving it?" Rebekah said.

"Not even a dent," Mark moaned. "I'm clueless."

"You know, there's something very familiar about the phrase 'jubilant feet,' but I can't quite put my finger on it," Rebekah said.

"Try Google," Elizabeth piped. "Google knows everything."

"That's a good idea, Elizabeth. It's worth a try," Mark said.

"Excuse me," Rebekah said. "I'll be back in a jiffy."

"Where you goin'?" Isaac asked.

"To get my laptop," she answered.

"What about the no-electronics-at-the-dinner-table rule?" Isaac reminded her.

"Oops. Sorry. I guess the Nancy Drew in me got a little carried away."

"Nancy Drew is a character in some old-timey, mystery books," Jacob explained.

"From way back in the olden days," Elizabeth added.

Rebekah wrinkled her nose at the kids. "Well, *after* dessert, we'll ask Google."

"What's for dessert, Mom?" Isaac said.

"Butterscotch pie," Rebekah said. "Compliments of your dear, *old* dad."

After butterscotch pie and vanilla ice cream, Rebekah opened the laptop and typed "jubilant feet" in the Google search bar.

"That's it! Now, I remember. Look at this, Mark." Rebekah turned the computer screen to face her dinner guest.

Mark read: "Battle Hymn of the Republic" Analysis, Stanza 4.

He sounded forth the trumpet
That shall never call retreat;
He is sifting out the hearts of men
Before the judgment seat.
Oh, be swift, my soul, to answer Him!
Be jubilant, my feet!
Our God is marching on!

"Wasn't the "Battle Hymn of the Republic" connected to the Civil War era?" he asked excitedly.

"That's right," Stephen said.

"It says here," Rebekah said, "that Julia Ward Howe wrote the hymn in November of 1861, six months after the Civil War began. *The Atlantic Monthly* published it on the front page the following February, 1862. Although used as the Battle Hymn for the Union cause, the song also held a deeper spiritual meaning. In this stanza, Mrs. Howe expressed concern for man's soul and the victory won by swiftly running to Jesus."

Jacob pulled out his hand-written copy. "Look, Mark. The riddle also says, 'be swift, my soul!'"

Mark leaned back in his chair. "I'm not believing this. Y'all are awesome. The answer must be tied to the Civil War."

"I think it's a pretty safe assumption," Stephen said.

Mark shook his head. "Wow! Thank you! Thank y'all so much."

REFLECTIONS

POINTS TO PONDER

Why do you think the Fickles made the no-electronics-at-the-table rule? _____

_____

_____

WHAT DOES GOD SAY?

"Understand this, my dear brothers and sisters: You must all be quick to listen, slow to speak, and slow to anger." (James 1:19)

"Fools think their own way is right, but the wise listen to others." (Proverbs 12:15)

"Anyone who listens to My teaching and follows it is wise, like a person who builds a house on solid rock." (Matthew 7:24)

LIVE WHAT YOU LEARN

Does your family have the no-electronics-at-the-table rule? YES NO

I challenge you to become a better listener. Try the no-electronics-at-the-table rule for three weeks. ☺

CHAPTER 8:
PAM HARPER

During practice the following Tuesday, Rebekah noticed a little girl beside a slender brunette hugging the end of the bleachers far apart from the other soccer moms.

"Good kick, Dustin," Rebekah cheered and clapped. "Woohoo!"

The smartly-dressed woman shot a suspicious look toward Rebekah, who smiled and waved. "Are you Dustin's mom?" she called.

The woman nodded but didn't return the smile. Rebekah slid closer. "Hi, I'm Rebekah Fickle, Jacob's mother. We enjoyed having Dustin over for the campout a couple of weeks ago."

"Thanks," she answered.

"And your name?"

"Oh, I'm sorry. I'm Pamela—Pam Harper—and this is my daughter, Kelly."

"Kelly, you are such a pretty young lady. What grade are you in?"

"Second," Kelly answered shyly.

"Second. That's a fun grade. Dustin said you guys moved here about a year ago. What brought you to Clear Creek?" Rebekah said.

"Work," Pam answered. "My husband...uh...he's away for a while, and we moved here with my job."

"Yeah, Dustin told us that your husband works at the Pentagon. His position sounds very important."

"The Pentagon?" Pam repeated wryly. "Is that what he told you? Try the penitentiary, Mrs. Fickle. My husband's in prison. Come on, Kelly. We need to go."

The woman abruptly stood up and grabbed Kelly's hand.

"Oh, Pam, I am so sorry. It must be very hard for you. Please know that I'll be praying for you and your family, and if there's anything we can do to help you, please don't hesitate to ask."

"Thanks. It is what it is. Come on, Kelly." Pam walked away quickly, half dragging the little girl behind her. "Hurry. Get in the car," she ordered.

"Why do we have to leave?" Kelly said. "Miss Rebekah seems nice. You need a friend, Mama."

Pam slowed her pace and kissed the golden head. Hard lines crisscrossing her forehead relaxed a bit. She attempted a smile. "She does seem nice, but I just wanted to take you to…uh, to get some ice cream."

"Oh, boy!" Kelly said and skipped ahead to the car.

The smile faded. Pam took a deep breath. "One day at a time," she murmured.

~

Rebekah washed the last dirty pot from dinner and handed it to Stephen to dry. "I met Dustin's mom and little sister at the soccer field this afternoon," she said.

"Oh, good. Did you have a chance to visit?" he asked.

"Just for a minute. Stephen, Dustin's dad isn't in the military. He's in *prison*."

Stephen said nothing as he dried the pan and placed it in the cabinet. Several quiet minutes passed. "It must be really hard for his family," he finally said. "And for him."

"I told Pam we'll pray for them and not to hesitate to ask if they need help," Rebekah said.

"We should make a real effort get to know the Harpers and invite them to church," he said.

"Maybe an invitation would be more appealing if we also invited them to Sunday lunch," Rebekah suggested.

"Good idea."

Back in his bedroom, Jacob hunkered over a small desk writing:

October 2, 2018

Dear Prof. Sparrow,

My name is Jacob Fickle. I am in the 7th grade at Clear Creek Middle School, and I am writing a research paper on the history of Clear Creek. My English teacher, Mrs. Culpepper, said that we have to interview a person that has lived in our town at least 25 years. May I interview you?

My address is:

5101 Mulberry Street, Clear Creek, IN 47403.

My email address is:

jfickle413@clearcreek.com.

I hope to hear from you soon.

Sincerely,

Jacob

He tucked the letter into an envelope and sealed it with a lick. *Lord, please help Professor Sparrow like my letter and let me interview him.*

~

Three days later, Professor Sparrow tossed the day's junk mail into the trash. From his favorite sunning spot on the window seal, Morton watched a letter slide from the bundle onto the floor. The old man stooped to pick up the hand-addressed envelope and pushed his glasses up on his nose.

"Jacob Fickle. Hmm. Do we know a Jacob Fickle, Morton?"

"Meow."

Using a polished-brass letter opener, he sliced the top of the envelope and scanned the lined, notebook paper. "Just a youngster. Seventh grader. He's writing a paper on the history of Clear Creek and wants to interview me because I'm *old*."

Professor Sparrow chuckled. "Little does he know that I hold the key to an unfathomable, historical discovery—far superior to Harvard's unearthing the long-lost copy of the Declaration of Independence, if I do say so myself."

"Meow."

REFLECTIONS

POINTS TO PONDER

Why do you think Dustin lied about his dad?

_____

Have you ever felt embarrassed or ashamed of yourself or someone you love?   YES   NO

WHAT DOES GOD SAY?

"For everyone has sinned; we all fall short of God's glorious standard." (Romans 3:23)

"If we claim we have no sin, we are only fooling ourselves and not living in the truth. But if we confess our sins to Him, He is faithful and just to forgive us our sins and to cleanse us from all wickedness." (1 John 1:8-9)

"His unfailing love toward those who fear Him is as great as the height of the heavens above the earth. He has removed our sins as far from us as the east is from the west." (Psalm 103:11-12)

LIVE WHAT YOU LEARN

Are you ashamed of something you said or did? Tell Jesus and receive His forgiveness. Remind yourself daily that absolutely nothing can separate you from God's love (Romans 8:38-39).

CHAPTER 9:
SMARTER THAN A FIFTH GRADER

Mark opened his laptop at the campus library. Every research trail he'd followed since dinner with the Fickles two weeks prior had hit a dead end.

"Okay. Let's try 'Clear Creek, Indiana: Civil War' one more time," he murmured. Mark typed in the search bar and hit enter. He read:

"During the American Civil War, although Indiana was a northern state, the small town of Clear Creek found herself in an allegiance tug-of-war between the Union cause and the deep southern roots of some of its citizens. Long after the war, it was discovered that a number of locals were involved in the Underground Railroad, a network of secret routes and safe houses that helped African Americans escape slavery. These slavery sympathizers, called abolitionists, included men and women, black and white, free and enslaved."

"Underground Railroad," he muttered. "Let's try 'Underground Railroad Safe Houses of Indiana.'"

"The Hoosier State has a rich history of Underground Railroad operations. Historians, using primary and secondary sources, have pinpointed numerous sanctuaries for fugitive slaves, which included homes, barns, cellars, churches, schools, and caves," he read. "Schools? Like Indiana University? Sweet!"

Mark smiled and rubbed his hands together. "Do I have a surprise for you, Professor Sparrow!"

He closed the laptop and threw on his backpack. Outside, Mark pedaled from the library to the athletic complex and sprinted to the locker room to change into running gear.

On the field, Coach Barnes took the team through fifteen minutes of range-of-motion stretching followed by core-strength exercises and an eight-minute trot around the polyurethane track to warm up muscles and increase heart rates. Next, the runners performed a series of acceleration drills with short jogs in between for recovery: 30 meters of walking lunges, 30 meters of straight-leg bounding, 40 meters of power skipping, 40 meters of side slides, 40 meters of triple jump running, and 40 meters of all out sprints.

The whistle blew. "Okay, men, give me five kilometers on the natural terrain course," Coach Barnes shouted.

The runners exited the track and field complex with Mark leading the pack. They passed the football stadium and the frat houses on Apple Street and turned north on Woodberry Lane toward the historic, president's mansion. The white, three-storied, stuccoed-brick structure loomed on their right. Its front façade panned five bays wide, and tall columns lined the hexastyle portico.

Past the mansion, the runners left the pavement and followed a meandering pathway through the arboretum and botanical gardens, a gallery of trees and flowers and shrubs. Tall scarlet oaks formed a brilliant, red canopy overhead and a few hardy ferns—survivors of the frosty, autumn nights—fringed the trail. Mark loved open-air, long-distance running and marveled at God's glorious creation. He sang softly as he ran:

"Come, let us sing to the LORD,
Let us shout joyfully to the Rock of our salvation.
Let us come to Him with thanksgiving.
Let us sing psalms of praise to Him.
For the LORD is God,
A great King above all gods.
He holds in His hands the depths of the earth

And the mightiest mountains.
The sea belongs to Him, for He made it.
His hands formed the dry land, too.
Come, let us worship and bow down.
Let us kneel before the Lord our Maker,
For He is our God.
We are the people He watches over,
The flock under His care."

~

Professor Sparrow's Friday lecture examined the post-Civil War changes in America. "Southern Reconstruction," he said, "faced the daunting task of rebuilding destroyed land, towns, and cities as well as developing a new system of labor to replace the shattered, slavery workforce. In the North, however, the economy boomed into an industrial revolution. Weapons, leather goods, iron production, and textiles grew and improved throughout the war and afterwards. European immigrants flocked to the free states. Transportation, particularly railroads, exploded…"

~

Mark lingered after class. He walked up to the professor and confidently announced, "Underground Railroad."

"I beg your pardon, Mr. Williams?"

"Underground Railroad," he repeated. "That's the answer to your riddle. *Oh, be swift, my soul, to answer Him! Be jubilant, my feet!* Battle Hymn of the Republic. Civil War. The Underground Railroad. The university was a safe house for the Underground Railroad."

Professor Sparrow's eyes narrowed to slits. A smile slowly unfurled across his craggy face. "And you, Mr. Williams, are absolutely...WRONG! Good day."

Mark's countenance fell like an under-cooked pound cake. "But...but it seems...it seems so logical."

"Logical?" Professor Sparrow purred. "Logical? You think it's *logical* that the long-unknown answer to my riddle would be a common historical fact? Every fifth grader in America knows about the Underground Railroad. Think deeper, Mr. Williams."

Mark stood outside room #507 contemplating. *If it's not the Underground Railroad, then...*

He hurried back into the classroom. "Professor Sparrow?" he called.

67

The room stood empty.

"Professor Sparrow?" Mark called again. "Where…but how…there's only one..." He glanced at his watch. *Core group. Gotta scoot,* he thought.

REFLECTIONS

POINTS TO PONDER

How do you think Mark felt when Professor Sparrow said that the Underground Railroad was the incorrect answer?

_____

Should he give up or keep trying? _____

WHAT DOES GOD SAY?

"One day Jesus told His disciples a story to show them that they should always pray and never give up." (Luke 18:1)

"Let us run with endurance the race God has set before us. We do this by keeping our eyes on Jesus, the champion who initiates and perfects our faith..." (Hebrews 12:1b-2)

"So, let's not get tired of doing what is good. At just the right time, we will reap a harvest of blessing if we don't give up." (Galatians 6:9)

LIVE WHAT YOU LEARN

Do you have something hard to do that makes you want to give up? YES NO

What does Jesus tell us in Luke 18:1? Always

_____ and _____ give up!

CHAPTER 10:
CROSSING LINES

"Who wants to say our opening prayer?" Mark asked.

Caleb raised his hand. "I'll do it. Dear Lord, thank You for this day, and thank You for the freedom to study the Bible together. Please help Mark teach us and please help us live what we learn. In Jesus' name, Amen."

"Thanks, Caleb. So, who memorized this week's Bible verse?" Mark asked.

Four hands raised.

"Good. Noah, will you quote Galatians 3:28, please?"

"There is no longer Jew or Gentile...uh, slave or free, male or female. For you are all...uh, you are all one in Christ Jesus," he recited.

Mark gave him a high five. "Great job, man. Okay, guys, open your Bibles to Galatians chapter three and let's look at the verse in context. In other words, let's read what comes before and after verse twenty-eight to help us understand it better. Jacob, will you read verse twenty-six, please?"

"For you are all children of God through faith in Christ Jesus," Jacob read.

"So, what's that verse saying? Is every person on earth a child of God?" Mark asked.

"Yes," Charlie said.

"You think so? Let's read it again: 'For you are all children of God *through faith in Christ Jesus*,'" Mark emphasized. "Paul tells us that not every person on earth is a child of God—every person is His creation but not necessarily His child. It's only faith in Jesus Christ that puts us into God's family. And who can become a child of God according to verse twenty-eight?"

"Anybody that has faith in Jesus," Trevor said.

"Absolutely, Trevor. Like the song we learned in preschool says: red, brown, yellow, black, and white— anyone. American or European, African or Japanese, rich or poor, any man, woman, or child who calls upon the name of the Lord Jesus Christ will be saved and becomes a child of Father God for all eternity," Mark explained. "Can you think of times in Scripture when Jesus reached across social or racial lines?"

Jacob raised his hand. "He called Matthew, a tax collector, to be one of His disciples, and everybody hated the tax collectors back then."

"Good, Jacob," Mark said. "Other instances?"

"He went to Zacchaeus' house for lunch," Charlie said and then bobbed his head from side to side singing, "Zacchaeus was a wee little man and a wee little man was…"

Noah punched his arm.

"Ouch," Charlie cried.

Mark laughed. "Okay, okay. One more?"

"When Jesus talked to the Samaritan woman at the well," Noah said.

"Good job, guys. So, what opportunities do you have to connect across racial and economic lines?"

Silence.

"It's okay to say it, guys," Mark encouraged. "Our core group is a perfect sample of friendships across different cultures and backgrounds. Jacob's white. Charlie is African American. Caleb's ancestors came from the middle east…"

"And you're from *Tennessee*," Jacob teased.

"Ha, ha," Mark said. "Now, on a more serious note, who do you know that may not be in God's family?"

"Our neighbors," Noah said.

"My grandparents," Caleb said.

"My friend, Dustin, and his family don't go to church," Jacob said.

"Does going to church or reading your Bible or praying everyday make you God's child?" Mark asked.

'No," the boys said in unison.

"What does?" Mark said.

"Faith in Jesus," they answered.

"Well, Dustin might be a Christian," Jacob said, "but he doesn't really act like it."

"Only God truly knows if a heart belongs to Him," Mark reminded.

"Mark," Trevor said, "what do you think happens to people when they die if they don't have a relationship with Jesus?"

"Well, Trevor," Mark answered, "Jesus said in Matthew 25:46 that those who reject Him will go into eternal punishment."

"You mean hell?" Trevor asked.

"But how can a loving God send good people to hell?" Caleb asked. "My grandparents may not believe in Jesus, but they're *really* good people."

"Well, Caleb, first of all, there are no inherently 'good' people. I know it's hard for us to wrap our minds around, but the truth is, all people are inherently sinful. Do you remember Romans 3:23? 'For *everyone* has sinned; we *all* fall short of God's glorious standard.' Every person born to earth arrives with a bent toward sin. Just think about it. Did anyone have to teach you to lie or disobey your parents or be selfish?"

"No," the boys answered.

"Me neither. We came into the world with a selfish, sinful nature. And second of all, our loving God does not *send* people to hell. On the contrary, God gave the ultimate sacrifice so that *all* people would have the opportunity to be in heaven with Him forever. He loved the whole world so much that He gave His Son for us. Can you even imagine that? God gave His one and only Son, Jesus, to die in our place—to take the punishment for the sins *we* committed. Jesus died as a ransom to set us free from the penalty of sin, and whoever believes on Him, *will* have everlasting life in heaven."

You could've heard a pin drop.

"You're right, Caleb. God is loving," Mark continued. "The Bible says He *is* love, but God is also holy and just. And He must deal justly with sin, or He wouldn't be holy. Jesus' death satisfied God's justice, but each person must *willingly* receive God's free gift of forgiveness and rescue—an invitation He extends to one and all. A person who rejects Jesus is choosing to pay for his own sins forever in the place of eternal punishment."

"Bad choices lead to bad consequences," Jacob said.

Caleb nodded soberly.

"I know today's lesson wasn't fun, guys, but it is very, *very* important. So, for our closing prayer today, instead of asking for our own needs and wants, let's pray for the people that may not know Jesus," Mark said. "Let's ask God to draw them unto Himself so they will experience the magnificent grace and holiness and love of God that we've experienced."

After the heartfelt prayer, Mark followed the boys' push-and-shove race up the steps.

REFLECTIONS

POINTS TO PONDER

John 3:16 says that God so loved the whole world that He gave Jesus. If God loves all people, how should we treat people that are different from us? _____

_____

WHAT DOES GOD SAY?

"For the LORD your God is God of gods and Lord of lords, the great God, mighty and awesome, who shows no partiality and cannot be bribed." (Deuteronomy 10:17)

"He Himself is the sacrifice that atones for our sins—and not only our sins but the sins of all the world." (I John 2:2)

"So now I am giving you a new commandment: Love each other. Just as I have loved you, you should love each other. Your love for one another will prove to the world that you are My disciples." (John 13:34-35)

LIVE WHAT YOU LEARN

This week look for someone that seems different or lonely and invite them to join you and your friends in the cafeteria or on the playground.

CHAPTER 11:
SAFE HOUSE

In the vestibule, Jacob bumped the shadow box hanging on the wall. "Sorry," he said and straightened the frame.

Mark said, "Okay, guys, settle down till we get outside. We don't wanna tear the place down."

"Look, Mark," Jacob said. "Today's memory verse."

"Where?"

"In this box thingamajig."

"That's the Church Charter, the official document issued to grant the people of Clear Creek the authority to establish Hebron Community Church dated…wow …April 3, 1829, before the Civil War," Mark said.

"See, Galatians 3:28 is down here at the bottom of a paper below the Charter." Jacob pointed to the Statement of Faith and read aloud:

We the founding fathers of Hebron Community Church believe that the Bible is the authoritative Word of God.

We believe in One God, eternally existing in three persons: Father, Son, and Holy Spirit.

We believe that Jesus Christ is God the Son, conceived by the Holy Spirit, born of the virgin, Mary. His death and shed blood on the cross atoned for our sins. On the third day, He rose from the dead, ascended to the right hand of the Father, and will one day return in power and glory.

We believe there is neither Jew nor Greek, there is neither bond nor free, there is neither male nor female; for all are one in Christ Jesus (Galatians 3:28).

Therefore, as the city of Hebron remained a Levitical refuge in the Kingdom of Israel, so shall Hebron Community Church forever remain a refuge in the great state of Indiana in these United States of America—a safe house for men, women, and children of every kindred, and tongue, and people, and nation. So, help us God.

"Mark," Jacob said, "doesn't this Statement of Faith kinda contradict what you taught us today? Hebron Community Church pledged to be a safe house for *all* people, but you said that only people that trust in Jesus can get to Father God in heaven."

Mark put a hand on Jacob's shoulder. "Well, the truth is, Jacob, Hebron's pledge and the Good News of Jesus Christ may seem like a contradiction at first glance, but, if you study Scripture carefully, their vow and the Gospel are actually in perfect harmony."

Mark opened his Bible to Romans chapter ten. "Look here. Verse nine teaches that if you confess with your mouth Jesus as Lord—which identifies 'Lord' as Jesus Christ—and believe in your heart that God raised Jesus from the dead, you will be saved. In other words, every person dead in his sins will be made alive in Christ, *when* he believes in Him. Verses twelve and thirteen go on to say that there is *no* distinction between Jew and Greek, for the same Lord Jesus is Lord of all. He's Lord for all, that is, *who will* call upon His name. So, the good people of Hebron Community Church served as a safe house and graciously opened their doors to anyone and everyone, giving *all* people the *opportunity* to hear this Good News: God's invitation to come to Him through one door—Jesus, His Son. Does that make sense?"

Jacob nodded. "Yeah, what you just said lines up with John 3:16 that God loved the *world* so much that He gave His one and only Son, that everyone who *believes* in Him will not perish but have eternal life."

"That's exactly right. In reality, Jesus is the true safe house...safe house," Mark repeated thoughtfully. "Hey, Jacob, will you ask your folks if I can come over sometime this weekend to talk about the riddle?"

"Sure."

~

Professor Sparrow climbed from the cellar puffing like a steam engine. His long hair stuck out in every direction like quills on a porcupine and perspiration trickled from his temples. Morton greeted him in the antiquated kitchen.

"Meow."

"Morton, ol' boy, (huff, puff). I'm getting too (huff) old (puff) for that," he wheezed.

A gingerbread clock on floral wallpaper chimed: BONG! BONG! BONG! BONG! BONG!

"Five o'clock already?" the professor marveled. "I've been down there over an hour? It used to take me only fifteen minutes."

Professor Sparrow pulled an oak chair from the kitchen table and plopped down. Morton rubbed against the chair leg and jumped into his friend's lap. The old man stroked the soft ears.

"Purrrrrrr."

"Mr. Williams came to see me after class today," the professor said. "Yes, he was quite certain that he'd solved the riddle (chuckle). He hasn't, of course, but the compass is pointed in the right direction."

"Meow."

REFLECTIONS

POINTS TO PONDER

At a time in history when deep-rooted prejudice plagued America, Hebron Community Church vowed to be a safe house for all people. Do you think their godly decision was easy or hard to carry out? _____

WHAT DOES GOD SAY?

"But even if you suffer for doing what is right, God will reward you for it. So don't worry or be afraid of their threats." (1 Peter 3:14)

"Remember, it is sin to know what you ought to do and not do it." (James 4:17)

"God blesses you when people mock you and persecute you and lie about you and say all sorts of evil things against you because you are My followers. Be happy...For a great reward awaits you in heaven..." (Matthew 5:11-12)

LIVE WHAT YOU LEARN

This week take advantage of opportunities to do the right thing—even if it's hard and unpopular with your friends.

CHAPTER 12:
HER

Jacob slammed the front door and bounded up the stairs. "Mom!" he called. "Did I get any mail today?"

In the kitchen, Rebekah stood with the phone to her ear and held up a finger for Jacob to wait a minute.

"Hi, Pam," she said, "this is Rebekah Fickle. We met at the boys' soccer practice a couple of weeks ago. I got your number from the realty agency. I have a question for you. Will you call me back when you have time, please? Thank you." Click.

"Did I get a letter from Professor Sparrow?" Jacob asked again.

"No, sorry, buddy. How was core group?"

"Fine," Jacob answered. "Mom, what am I going to do? It's been two weeks since I mailed that letter, and he still hasn't answered. This research thing is way too hard."

"Hard is good," Rebekah said.

"Huh?"

"Having something hard to do is a good thing because it makes us depend on God more than ourselves. Just be patient, Jacob, and trust God. He led you to help

Mark, so I'm sure He'll help you, as well," Rebekah reassured him. "God who calls you is faithful, and He will do it just like it says in 1 Thessalonians 5:24. In the meantime, keep searching the internet and those books you got from the library."

"Oh, I almost forgot," Jacob said. "Mark asked if he could come over sometime this weekend to talk about the riddle."

"Sure, let me talk to your dad to figure out the best time."

Rebekah's phone rang.

"It's Pam Harper!" she said excitedly. "Hi, Pam. Thanks for calling me back so quickly."

"Hi, Rebekah. Is there something I can help you with? Are you selling your home or hoping to buy a new one?" Pam said.

Rebekah laughed. "No, nothing like that. We were just wondering if you and Dustin and Kelly would like to go to church with us on Sunday and then join us for lunch afterwards at our house. It won't be anything fancy, but we'd love to have you."

"Umm, where and what time?"

"We go to the 11 o'clock service at Hebron Community Church."

"Uh," Pam hesitated, "I don't think we can make it, but thanks."

"Maybe another time," Rebekah said. "See you at the game tomorrow?"

"I'm working," Pam said.

"Oh, okay. Well, have a nice weekend, and I hope we can get together soon."

"Thanks. Bye." Click.

Rebekah turned to Jacob. "Since the Harpers aren't coming, I'll ask your dad if Sunday lunch is a good time for Mark to come over. Don't worry, Jacob. Everything will work out. You'll see."

~

On Sunday, Rebekah lifted the lid from a crockpot and tasted the soup. "Elizabeth, honey," she said, "will you set the table, please?"

The bare-footed girl danced and twirled as she placed forks, knives, and spoons beside blue dinner plates.

"Where are your shoes, young lady?" her mother said.

Elizabeth grinned.

"May I help, Mrs. Fickle?" Mark asked.

Rebekah handed him a paring knife and an amber, glass bowl. "Do you mind slicing these apples and putting them in here? I hope you like vegetable-beef soup."

"It smells great." He cut an apple and popped a crisp slice into his mouth.

"This meal was a favorite at my house when I was a girl—homemade vegetable-beef soup, buttermilk cornbread, cheese slices, and apple wedges," Rebekah said. "Soup or chili tastes so good when the weather turns cool."

"What's your family like, Mrs. Fickle?"

Rebekah chattered happily about her parents and brothers in Alabama. "Daddy bought some land on the Coosa River a

few years ago. So, now, he's a forester and a farmer." She laughed. "Jacob stayed with them for a week last summer, and he and Daddy built a treehouse in the woods on their property."

"That sounds like fun," Mark said.

"Yeah, it was. We'd work a while and then ride jet skis awhile," Jacob said. "And I learned to wakeboard."

"That's awesome," Mark said.

Elizabeth stuck out her lip. "Isaac and I didn't get to go."

"Maybe next year, baby. Like I was saying, I have two brothers, Ben and Dan, and two of the sweetest sisters-in-law ever, and three, adorable nephews: Alexander, Hunter, and Lee."

"Yeah, and Aunt Amanda's having another baby boy any day now," Elizabeth chimed in.

A bright smile stretched across Rebekah's pretty face. "Another nephew! We're all *so* excited!

"I'm sure you miss your family," Mark said.

"Yes, I do, but I know God has good purposes for us in Indiana—especially through Stephen's work at the church," Rebekah said. "Stephen, the cornbread's ready.

Will you dip the soup, please? Anyway, Stephen and I met the first day of seventh grade and became instant best friends, and…oh, I'm sorry. That's probably *way* more information than you cared to hear."

"Not at all. I love hearing people's stories," Mark said.

At the table, all joined hands and Stephen prayed, "God, thank You so much for this beautiful day. Thank You for Reverend Wheeler and his challenging message this morning. Thank You for Mark and what He means to our family, and we thank You for this food. We love You so much, Jesus. In Your name we pray, Amen."

"Amen," Mark said.

"So, Mark," Stephen said, "Jacob said you want to talk about the riddle."

"Yes, sir, and I also wanted to ask Jacob how his research is coming along. Maybe we can compare notes and make some headway in solving this thing."

"Well, I wrote Professor Sparrow a letter and asked if I could interview him, but he hasn't answered," Jacob said.

"I'd be shocked if he does," Mark said. "At school, he doesn't seem very friendly or overly eager to help students. I have another idea for you, Jacob, but first, did you tell your mom and dad about our discovery at the church?"

"No."

Rebekah's blue eyes sparkled like the sun-kissed sea. "What did you find???"

"Well, I really believe we're on the right track as far as the mystery being connected to the Clear Creek Civil War days. I learned that Indiana was heavily involved in the Underground Railroad to help slaves escape to freedom and sometimes schools were used as secret safe houses. I thought that the Underground Railroad was the answer to the riddle, but Professor Sparrow said that I was wrong. But then, at the church, the boys and I discovered that Hebron Community Church was established before the Civil War and that the founding fathers resolved that it would remain a *safe house* for all people regardless of race or gender or economic status. So, I have a hunch that the church may be tied to the professor's secret."

"Is there something in the riddle that leads you to believe it's connected to the church?" Stephen asked.

"Line six: *To comfort her travail*," Mark said, "because what is the church called in chapter nineteen of Revelation?"

"Chapter nineteen, let me think. The Bride of Christ? No, I know, the Lamb's bride!" Rebekah said.

"Exactly. So, couldn't 'her' in the riddle be the church? It says be brave and bold to comfort 'her' travail and couldn't that possibly mean to comfort the church's sorrow?" he continued eagerly. "And what would have caused the church travail or deep sorrow during the Civil War?"

"Brothers and sisters in Christ fighting against one another," Stephen said.

"Absolutely!" Mark exclaimed. "So, I believe we need to figure out what happened during the Civil War that brought Hebron Community Church comfort. If it wasn't the Underground Railroad, then what was it? And, Jacob, my idea is to interview Rev. Wheeler instead of Professor Sparrow. The pastor's family has lived in Clear Creek for decades."

"That's a great idea! Can we call him now, Dad?" Jacob said.

"Let's not disturb the pastor on Sunday afternoon. Why don't you contact him at his office tomorrow?" Stephen suggested.

"I'll call Rev. Wheeler if you want me to, Jacob," Mark volunteered.

"Yeah!" Jacob said.

"Hold on, Bud," Stephen said. "It's your responsibility to find your resources for the paper. *You* need to call."

"Okay," Jacob said.

"Why don't you ask Rev. Wheeler if he can meet with us on Wednesday night after the midweek service. Will that work for you, Jacob?" Mark said.

"Sure. I'll call him after school tomorrow."

REFLECTIONS

POINTS TO PONDER

Jacob's mom said that having something hard to do is good because it helps us depend on God more than ourselves. What is hard for you to do? _____

_____

WHAT DOES GOD SAY?

"For I hold you by your right hand—I, the LORD your God. And I say to you, 'Don't be afraid. I am here to help you!'" (Isaiah 41:13)

"For I can do everything through Christ, who gives me strength." (Philippians 4:13)

Jesus replied, "What is impossible for people is possible with God." (Luke 18:27)

LIVE WHAT YOU LEARN

Ask God now (and keep on asking Him) to help you do things that are hard for you.

CHAPTER 13:
MISS ALICE

Dustin caught up with Jacob in the hallway between first and second period on Monday morning.

"Hey, Dustin," Jacob said.

"Whatcha doin' this weekend?" he asked.

"Just soccer on Saturday and church on Sunday. Why?"

Dustin looked both ways and whispered, "I've got a huge garbage bag full of toilet paper stashed in the closet at my house. Wanna meet me at Professor Sparrow's Friday night and roll his yard?"

Jacob answered curtly, "No."

"Why not? You scared? Chicken! Puk-puk-pukaaak!" Dustin clucked and flapped his arms like a laying hen.

"Nope, I'm smart. The last time you talked me into sneaking off in the night, I got grounded for two weeks and missed Caleb's party," Jacob said.

"Suit yourself. Hey, Noah," Dustin called, "wait up."

~

On Wednesday after prayer meeting, a silver-haired gentleman in his seventies welcomed Mark and Jacob into his office with a warm smile and a firm handshake. "Have a seat, boys. How may I help you this evening?"

"You tell him, Mark," Jacob said.

"Okay. Well, first of all, thank you, Rev. Wheeler, for meeting with us tonight. It's kind of a long story, but we'll try to make it as brief as possible. Jacob is working on a research paper for his seventh-grade English class, and I'm trying to solve an American-history riddle from Professor Sparrow at the university. And Jacob is…well, actually, all the boys in my core group are helping me," Mark explained.

"Benjamin Sparrow," Rev. Wheeler repeated and chuckled.

Mark's eyebrows raised. "You know him?"

"Yes, we've met on a few occasions over the years." The pastor went on to tell them about growing up on a farm just south of Clear Creek and leaving in the 1960s to go to Old College Seminary at Notre Dame. "When I returned to Clear Creek as senior pastor of Hebron Community Church, Ben Sparrow had just moved to town. I tried my best to get that man through the doors of the sanctuary but never succeeded. A strange bird that Professor Sparrow—brilliant mind, excellent teacher, one of the top American-history scholars in the nation. But you just have to wonder what's ticking behind that academic mask. What drives a man into utter seclusion like that?" Rev. Wheeler shook his head. "Oh, sorry, boys. You were saying about your projects?"

Mark handed the pastor the riddle. "Our research leads us to believe that Hebron Community Church played a part in the mystery, and we're hoping that maybe you can help us put the pieces of the puzzle together."

"I see," Rev. Wheeler said. He read and reread the lyric. "So, what are your theories so far?"

Jacob answered, "We think the phrases *be swift, my soul* and *be jubilant feet* point to the "Battle Hymn of the Republic" and the Civil War. And Mark thinks that the *her* in line six is the church—this church."

Mark scooted to the edge of his seat. "The Statement of Faith out in the vestibule says that the founding fathers vowed that Hebron Community Church would be a refuge or safe house for all people regardless of race, gender, or economic status, which was highly abnormal in that day and time. So, Rev. Wheeler, we were just wondering, was this church a safe house for the Underground Railroad?"

"Boys, this mystery is certainly fascinating. I'm really impressed with your investigation and enthusiasm, but I'm afraid I just don't know the answers to your questions."

Hope withered like the dry, autumn leaves. Jacob groaned.

"However, I *do* know someone who might—our church historian, Alice Holtshausen. In fact, she's probably still here. Let's go see."

The threesome hurried to the sanctuary. Clusters of chatting parishioners filled the hardwood aisle and spaces between curved pews. "There she is." Rev. Wheeler nodded toward a bent figure leaning on a wooden cane.

"Miss Alice, these two, young men would like to meet you," Rev. Wheeler called.

Clear, hazel eyes greeted them and a crinkled hand patted Jacob's arm. "How delightful. What's your name, young man?"

"Jacob Fickle."

Her smile widened. "You must be Rebekah and Stephen's boy."

"Yes, ma'am," he answered.

"And, Miss Alice, I'm Mark Williams, a student at Indiana University. It's such a pleasure to meet you," he said. "Go ahead, Jacob. Ask our question."

"We were wondering if Hebron Community Church was a safe house for the Underground Railroad during the Civil War," Jacob said.

"Quite a timeworn question for such youthful minds," she commented.

"Jacob's doing research for an English paper," Rev. Wheeler explained, "and Mark's trying to solve Professor Sparrow's history riddle at IU."

"Ah, Professor Sparrow. May we sit down, gentlemen?" Miss Alice said.

"Of course," Mark said. He took her elbow and guided her to an empty pew.

"To answer your question, in a sense, yes, this church was a safe house during the Civil War."

"I knew it!" Mark exclaimed.

"But not for the Underground Railroad."

Mark's brow furrowed. "I don't understand."

97

"The church was openly a welcoming safe house of refuge for *all* people—*any* man, woman, or child, white or black, rich or poor. And even more astounding, the congregation uniquely ministered to both Union *and* Confederate supporters. When the war broke out between the states, Reverend Jeremiah Walvoord and his elders resolved that Hebron Community Church would refuse help to no one—regardless of which side of the Mason-Dixon line held their hearts."

"This information is astounding," Mark said. "We read about their resolution to help all people in the church's Statement of Faith, but what did that look like? How did they get away with helping both Northerners and Southerners?"

"Much of the story's told in the journal," she answered.

"What journal?" Jacob said.

"Did Reverend Wheeler tell you boys that my great-great-grandfather—my Grandmother Murphey's grandfather— was one of the church's founding fathers?"

The pastor smiled. "I'm afraid I neglected to tell them that interesting fact, Miss Alice."

"Yes, Grandfather Watts was a founding father, and he left a detailed journal recording the church's courageous acts of kindness as well as the attacks of severe opposition they encountered prior to and during the War Between the States. But it's a long story, and it's getting rather late. This young lady needs her beauty sleep," she said with an amused smile. "May we get together another time?"

"Yes, ma'am, please!" Mark said. "Our core group meets in the basement on Friday afternoons. Could you meet with us this Friday at 4:00? I'd love for all the guys to hear your amazing story."

"May I come, too?" Rev. Wheeler asked.

REFLECTIONS

POINTS TO PONDER

Miss Alice is an elderly woman. Do you think old people are a valuable asset or an inconvenient liability to a community? _____ Why?_____

_____

WHAT DOES GOD SAY?

"Wisdom belongs to the aged and understanding to the old." (Job 12:12)

"Stand up in the presence of the elderly and show respect for the aged. Fear your God. I am the Lord." (Leviticus 19:32)

"But the godly will flourish like palm trees and grow like the cedars of Lebanon. Even in old age they will still produce fruit; they will remain vital and green. They will declare, 'The LORD is just! He is my Rock! There is no evil in Him!'" (Psalm 92:12,14-15)

LIVE WHAT YOU LEARN

If you have living grandparents or know someone over 50 years of age, ask them questions like:

1. What's the most valuable lesson you have ever learned?

2. What advice would you give a kid my age?

3. If you could live life over again, what would you do differently?

CHAPTER 14:
SQUIGGLES

Early Friday at 6:30 a.m., Rebekah picked up her ringing cell phone and saw "Dan" on caller ID.

"It's Dan!" she cried excitedly. "Maybe the baby's here."

Elizabeth squealed.

Rebekah turned on speakerphone. "Hi, Dan. What's up?"

"You have a new nephew," Rebekah's youngest brother said.

"Congratulations!" Rebekah shouted over the background uproar. "You can tell from all the shouts, squeals, barks, and tweets that everyone's excited, even the pets. Tell us everything."

Dan described the night's adventure beginning with Amanda going into labor shortly after midnight and ending with baby Daniel's birth only two hours after a fast ride to the hospital. "He weighs eight pounds. He's twenty-one inches long and has a head full of black hair," he said.

"Black hair! You're kidding," Rebekah exclaimed. "All the other kids in the family were practically bald."

"Not this one."

"How's Amanda?"

"Tired, but she's doing well," Dan said.

Stephen called from the kitchen, "I guessed the weight right on the nose."

"Yep, eight pounds. And Gabriela got the birth date, October 26th," Dan said.

"We can't wait to meet baby Daniel and see all of you when we're in Alabama for Christmas," Rebekah said.

"He'll be two months old by then."

"I know. I wish Indiana and Alabama were closer. Maybe we can do some FaceTime."

"That's a good idea. Well, I know y'all need to get ready for work and school, but I just wanted to tell you the good news. Y'all got the first call since you're on eastern time. It's only 5:30 here. I'll call Ben's family in a little while."

"Send lots of pictures! We love all of you so much, and please send our love to Amanda and tell her congratulations," Rebekah said.

"Will do. Love y'all, too. G'bye."

"Bye, bye."

"Another boy," Jacob said. "Now Papaw and Mamaw Willowkins have six grandboys and only one grandgirl."

Elizabeth grinned. "I *like* being the only girl.

"Okay, kiddos," Rebekah said, "run eat your breakfast and get dressed for school."

~

That afternoon, on the fifth floor of the history building, Mark slipped from Professor Sparrow's class a few minutes early so as not to be late for core group. Outside, bright sunshine set the campus ablaze. Mammoth trees in brilliant colors lined the walkways. Orange, gold, and crimson mums overflowed large urns, and the beds surrounding the old, stone buildings exploded with purple and yellow pansies.

IU must be one of the prettiest colleges in the country, Mark thought, *especially this time of year.*

103

At the church, he found Miss Alice on the front steps with a flock of early arrivers listening attentively to the enchanting guest of honor.

"Ah, here he is," Miss Alice said. "Nice bike."

Mark gave her a warm hug. "Thanks. It's my 'car' from the parents. I'm so glad you could come today."

"I was just telling the boys about the cornerstone. It's the special piece of the architecture that the masons set first, you know, to determine the position of the entire structure. Like I was saying, cornerstones often provide important information about the building, but this one will fascinate you. Follow me, gentlemen."

Miss Alice hobbled to the right side of the church and pushed back the boxwoods. "Here it is—dated April 21, 1829. Construction began just a couple of weeks after the Church Charter was signed. See those marks?"

Mark studied the strange insignia below the date:

מר אחז י

"What does it mean?" asked Jacob.

"I don't know," Miss Alice said. "It must be some sort of secret message shared by the founding fathers. Come on; there's more. You have to see what's in the cemetery."

"Are you sure, Miss Alice?" Mark asked. "It's a pretty long walk."

She linked elbows the cross-country athlete. "Oh, I may be old and slow, but I can still outwalk you, young man."

When the rest of the boys showed up, Rev. Wheeler emerged from the office to join the pack. Miss Alice held tightly to Mark's arm and led the caravan through the tall gates. Golden sugar maples and giant, copper-topped bur oaks peppered the manicured cemetery. In a back corner lined with weathered tombstones, Miss Alice paused and studied the monuments.

"Hmm...over here, I think." She walked further down the row and pointed to a simple marker. It read:

In loving memory of
Asa Hartford Watts
Born: December 23, 1795
Died: June 5, 1871
מר אחי

"Here it is," she said. "This is my great-great-grandfather's gravesite."

"Look!" Caleb exclaimed, "those same weird squiggles."

Miss Alice said, "And you'll find them on each of the founding fathers' headstones and Rev. Walvoord's as well. That's what I wanted to show you."

"Those 'weird squiggles' as you called them, Caleb, are Hebrew letters," Rev. Wheeler said. "Did you boys know that Hebrew is written from right to left?"

Everyone gaped at the pastor.

"You know Hebrew?" Jacob said. "What does it mean?"

"I'm sorry. I wish I could tell you. It's just been too long. I know it's Hebrew letters, but I can't translate them anymore. Mark, I'm sure one of the professors in the religion department at IU could tell you what this means."

Mark grabbed a piece of paper and a pencil from his backpack and knelt beside the headstone. Pressing the paper firmly against the hard surface, he rubbed the side of the pencil lead across the writing. The Hebrew phrase appeared on the paper.

"Oh, cool!" Charlie said.

"And here's my great-great-grandmother's grave," Miss Alice said, indicating the headstone adjacent to Asa Watts.

Beloved wife and mother
Alma Merriweather Watts
Born: April 10, 1799
Died: June 20, 1877

Mark took Miss Alice by the hand. "This information is incredible, Miss Alice," he said. "What about the old journal you mentioned?"

She patted her pocketbook. "Got it right here. Let's go back to the sanctuary."

REFLECTIONS

POINTS TO PONDER

Miss Alice showed the boys the cornerstone of the church building. In the Bible, who is called the Cornerstone? _____ (answer found in the Scriptures below).

WHAT DOES GOD SAY?

"Give thanks to the LORD, for His is good! His faithful love endures forever. The Stone that the builders rejected has now become the cornerstone." (Psalm 118:1,22)

"For Jesus is the one referred to in Scripture, where it says, 'The stone that you builders rejected has now become the cornerstone.' There is salvation in no one else! God has given no other name under heaven by which we must be saved." (Acts 4:11-12)

"Together, we are His house, built on the foundation of the apostles and the prophets. And the cornerstone is Christ Jesus Himself. We are carefully joined together in Him, becoming a holy temple for the Lord." (Ephesians 2:20-21)

LIVE WHAT YOU LEARN

How can you build your life upon Jesus, the Cornerstone? Read Romans 10:9 and Colossians 2:7.

_____

_____

Chapter 15:
The Journal

Mark and the boys filled the front pew of the beautiful, old sanctuary. Rev. Wheeler set a chair for Miss Alice facing the squirming youngsters.

"Grandfather Watt's journal is too long to read in its entirety," she began, "and too precious to let out of my sight. So, I selected a few key passages to share with you gentlemen today."

The journal smelled of mothballs like the hope chest where Miss Alice stored it for safe keeping. Gnarled hands opened the cracked, brown leather and gently smoothed the tattered pages. A faded signature verified Asa Hartford Watts' ownership. Water-blotched ink lined the fragile paper; jagged edges told the story of missing pages. In her mind's eye, Miss Alice relived the day the precious keepsake became hers.

~

It was April 6, 1944, Alice's eleventh birthday. "Alice," Grandmother Murphey had said, "you must take very special care of this old diary, dear. It was my Grandfather Watts' journal, a treasure book of his hopes and dreams, wisdom and integrity, successes and sorrows, plans and *secrets*."

Young Alice wrapped her arms tightly around thin shoulders and kissed her grandmother's soft cheek. "Oh, thank you, Grandma! I'll cherish it forever and always."

~

"Miss Alice?" Rev. Wheeler repeated, snapping her back to the present.

"Oh, uh, what? I'm sorry," she said.

"Miss Alice, why don't you tell the boys where your great-great-grandfather lived," Rev. Wheeler said.

"Of course. Grandfather Watt's built the old mansion on Rabbit Road where Benjamin Sparrow now lives," she said.

Mark jumped to his feet. "Professor Sparrow lives in Asa Watts' house—a founding father of this church?"

"Yes, Mark, now sit down please and listen."

"Yes, ma'am."

The boys giggled. Mark sat down. Miss Alice read:

Sunday, July 4, 1858.

Tonight, after the Independence Day picnic on the grounds, Rev. Walvoord met privately with the elders of Hebron Community Church. He relayed the solemn news that our nation hangs in the balance between peace and the sword and quoted Senator Abraham Lincoln of Illinois as saying:

"A house divided against itself cannot stand. I believe this government cannot endure permanently half slave and half free. I do not expect the Union to be dissolved. I do not expect it to fall, but I do expect it will cease to be divided. It will become all one thing or all the other."'

I shall never forget Rev. Walvoord's sobering question: "Gentlemen, will thou love thy neighbor as thyself should war break out between the northern and southern states of America?"

Thus, the elders unanimously agreed to raise a workforce to carry out the great commission bestowed upon Christ's church. We shall share the Good News of salvation through faith in Jesus Christ and provide help and refuge for all peoples of every race or creed. Therefore, the secret mission begins tomorrow—Mission-T, an unquestionably impossible task for man alone but unquestionably doable for God and man together.

Jacob raised his hand. "Miss Alice, what was Mission-T?"

Miss Alice shook her head. "Honestly, child, I don't know. It was…well, a secret, and my grandfather never disclosed the details of Mission-T in the journal. But I've been thinking that perhaps it had something to do with Professor Sparrow's riddle. Listen to this brief entry penned three years later, just days before the first mortar fired on Fort Sumter, April 12, 1861."

Friday, April 4, 1861.

The men are working selflessly day and night. Mission-T is nearing completion. A stockade of medical supplies, food, and water is in place. By the Lord's grace, we are ready for whatever the future holds. So, help us God.

"And in another passage two years into the war…" She read:

Wednesday, July 8, 1863.

Confederate troops are marching across Indiana. Today, the servants at Mission-T fed five hungry families and attended three injured soldiers, two Union and one Confederate.

"How inspiring!" Rev. Wheeler said. "Those men and women were awfully brave to minister to soldiers from both sides of enemy armies."

"*The truth that hides from modern eyes of ones so brave and bold*! Those are the last lines in Professor Sparrow's riddle. Hmmm. Mission-T. What was it?" Mark pondered. "The journal read *at* Mission-T. So, it must have been a place, but *where* was it?"

"Put the clues from Grandfather's journal together, Mark," Miss Alice advised. "He said that

Mission-T involved men working day and night for nearly three years, and it was well stocked with supplies to minister to people of the north *and* the south."

"Mission-Trouble?" Caleb guessed.

Rev. Wheeler said, "Good idea, Caleb, but that doesn't seem fitting for a labor force working day and night."

"And it doesn't explain the secrecy," Mark added.

"Don't give up boys. God says in Galatians 6:9: 'Let's not get tired of doing good. At just the right time, we will reap a harvest of blessing if we don't give up.' Keep digging. You'll solve this mystery yet. I just know it," Miss Alice encouraged.

"Thank you, Miss Alice, and thank you so much for coming today." Mark glanced at his watch. "Wow, where has the time gone? Charlie, will you say our closing prayer today, please?"

REFLECTIONS

POINTS TO PONDER

In a speech prior to his presidency, Senator Abraham Lincoln said, "A house divided against itself cannot stand." Do you feel like your home (your family) is divided or united? _____

WHAT DOES GOD SAY?

Jesus said, "Any kingdom divided by civil war is doomed. A town or a family splintered by feuding will fall apart." (Matthew 12:25)

"I appeal to you, dear brothers and sisters, by the authority of our Lord Jesus Christ, to live in harmony with each other. Let there be no divisions in the church. Rather, be of one mind, united in thought and purpose." (1 Corinthians 1:10)

"Do all that you can to live in peace with everyone." (Romans 12:18)

LIVE WHAT YOU LEARN

When you're in a disagreement or have angry feelings toward someone, *you* make the first move toward reconciliation (mending the relationship). Remember, a healthy relationship is more important than proving you are right.

115

CHAPTER 16:
STAKEOUT

After supper, Jacob lingered in the kitchen.

"Something on your mind, Bud?" Stephen asked.

"Dad," Jacob said.

"Yeah, Bud?"

"I need to tell you something," he admitted.

"What's up," Stephen asked.

Jacob said, "I think Dustin and some other guys are going to roll Professor Sparrow's house tonight."

"Really?" Stephen said. "What makes you think that?"

"Because Dustin asked me to go with him," Jacob explained. "It's kinda funny when kids roll each other's yard, but Professor Sparrow's really old and lives alone, and I think it would be hard on him."

"That's very considerate, Jacob. What do you think you should do about it?"

"Well, I was thinking that maybe you and Mark and I could stop 'em," Jacob said.

"How?"

"Go to Professor Sparrow's house and catch 'em before they make a big mess."

"That plan won't make you very popular with Dustin and the other guys," his dad said.

"I know, but I think it's the right thing to do."

"Me, too, son. Here. Use my phone and call Mark."

Jacob grinned. "Thanks, Dad."

Forty-five minutes later, Mark rang the doorbell.

"Thanks for coming, Mark," Stephen said. "Come on in."

"Hey, Jacob. So, what's the plan?" Mark asked.

"Go over to Professor Sparrow's house and wait for Dustin, I guess," Jacob said.

Mark said, "And what's the plan if they come?"

"Mmm, not sure. What do you think?" Jacob said.

"I think we should ask God."

"I agree," Stephen said. "Since this is your deal, Jacob, why don't you pray?"

"Sure. Dear Lord, thank You for this night, and thank You for my dad and Mark. Please help us know what to do and what to say if Dustin and the other guys come to Professor Sparrow's house, and please help them choose to do the right thing. In Jesus' name I pray, Amen."

"Amen," Stephen and Mark echoed.

"Okay, guys, let's go," Stephen said.

Two blocks southwest on Mulberry Lane, Jacob led the "posse" down the shortcut through the woods—a deer trail under trees and bushes—to Church Street. On Church Street, the threesome passed Clear Creek Cemetery and Hebron Community Church and then crossed the bridge onto Rabbit Road.

"Turn off your flashlights," Stephen whispered. "We're almost to Professor Sparrow's."

Mark pointed to thick shrubs beside the tall, front gates. "Come on," he whispered. "Let's hide over there."

Jacob chuckled. "I feel like I'm on a police stakeout."

Overhead, a half-moon played hide and seek behind rolling clouds, and a stiff breeze rattled branches and dry leaves. Stephen studied the stormy sky. "Hope it doesn't rain," he whispered.

Mark softly crooned:

> *"Rivers of living water,*
> *Rivers that flow from the throne,*
> *Rivers o'erflowing with blessing,*
> *Coming from Jesus alone."*

Jacob muffled a laugh. "Look!" He pointed up the road.

Three tiny lights bobbed in the distance.

"Somebody's coming," Mark whispered. "And the plan is?"

Stephen shrugged and looked at Jacob.

"Don't look at me," Jacob whispered. "You're the grownups."

Voices moved closer, and Jacob recognized Dustin's.

"Here," Dustin whispered, "loosen the end, like this, and then throw the roll up as high in the trees as you can."

"That house is creepy," whispered another familiar voice.

Mark and Jacob exchanged knowing looks. Mark jumped to his feet and shined a flashlight into three pairs of wide eyes.

"Hi, Noah," he said, "what are you doing out here tonight, and who are your friends?"

Dustin and another boy Jacob didn't recognize turned to run, but Jacob shouted, "Hey, Dustin. I'd like

119

for you to meet our core group leader. This is Mark, and you already know my dad."

Professor Sparrow's old house suddenly lit up like a Christmas tree and a crackly voice screeched, "What's going on out there?"

"Hey, Professor Sparrow," Mark called. "It's me, Mark Williams. Some of the core-group guys from church and I are just out for a walk."

"This time of night? In the dark? At my house?" the professor barked.

On a whim, Jacob yelled, "Yes, sir. We're looking for Mission-T. I'm Jacob Fickle—the one that wrote you a letter."

Silence.

"May I talk to you sometime, sir?" Jacob shouted.

Silence.

"Please?"

More silence.

"I really need to talk to you," he called again.

"I'll think about it," Professor Sparrow roared and slammed the front door. The old man ambled to the parlor and dropped into a leather chair beside an ornately-carved fireplace. The wood crackled and hissed. He stared at orange flames licking oak logs.

"Mission-T? Humph," he muttered. "It isn't possible. No way. They couldn't have."

"Meow," Morton bawled as he dug his sharp claws into the oriental rug.

~

On Rabbit Road, Stephen said, "Okay, boys, show's over. Dustin, we'll walk you home."

"You gonna tell my mom?" Dustin asked.

"No," Stephen answered. "You are."

Mark fell into stride with Noah. "Wanna tell me what you were doing out here tonight?"

Noah shrugged. "Just having some fun—a practical joke. We never meant to hurt anybody."

"So," Mark said, "do you think a rolled yard would've been fun for Professor Sparrow?"

Noah avoided Mark's gaze. "Guess not," he muttered.

"I understand this charade was Dustin's idea," Mark continued. "Do you think coming tonight was a good decision, Noah—one that honored God and respected your parents?"

"When you put it that way, no."

Up ahead, Dustin growled, "Great friend you are, Jacob."

Jacob countered, "A real friend cares about the decisions you make."

"You're weird," Dustin spewed. "And what was all that Mission-T stuff you were yellin' about?"

"It's a mystery us guys in core group are helping Mark solve. You should come to our meeting sometime. It's cool," Jacob said.

"What kind of mystery?" he asked.

"Come to core group and find out. We meet on Fridays at 4:00 in the basement of Hebron Community Church. And, by the way, who's the guy over there with my dad?'

"Oh, that's Braden. Just a neighbor."

Dustin stopped in front of a two-story duplex. Identical units lined Godfrey Avenue like a straight row of red-brick dominoes. A paint-chipped sign read: Creekside Apartments.

"This is it, Mr. Fickle." he said.

"Do I need to come in with you, Dustin?" Stephen asked.

"No, sir. I'll tell Mom," he promised. "Come on guys."

"What about you two, Noah and Braden? Do your parents know where you are?" Stephen said.

"I'm spending the night with Dustin," Noah said.

"I live here," Braden said.

"Well, good night, guys," Mark said.

Jacob called, "See you at the game tomorrow. Nice meeting you, Braden."

After Dustin and his "partners in crime" disappeared, Mark slapped Jacob on the back. "Good job, dude."

REFLECTIONS

POINTS TO PONDER

Was Jacob a good friend to Dustin or a bad friend when he stopped him from rolling Professor Sparrow's yard?

_____

_____

WHAT DOES GOD SAY?

"Wounds from a sincere friend are better than many kisses from an enemy." (Proverbs 27:6)

"Dear brothers and sisters, if another believer is overcome by some sin, you who are godly should gently and humbly help that person back on the right path. And be careful not to fall into the same temptation yourself." (Galatians 6:1)

"Let us think of ways to motivate one another to acts of love and good works." (Hebrews 10:24)

LIVE WHAT YOU LEARN

Jacob told Dustin that a good friend cares about the decisions you make. Resolve to be a good friend by encouraging your friends to make good decisions and discouraging them from doing wrong.

CHAPTER 17:
THE MESSAGE

At the soccer game the next morning, the Cougars trailed the Jets one to zero at half-time. To Jacob's relief, Dustin acted as if Friday night had never happened.

"Okay, guys, bring it in," Coach Tom shouted. "Hydrate and listen up. Way to hustle defense." He turned to the goalkeeper. "Tripp, they're launching those shots like missiles. Only one slipped by you; good work. Stay on your toes."

"Yes, sir."

"Offense, they're beating you to the ball. I need you to get there first. Dustin, play your position."

"Yes, sir."

"The Jets are good, but so are we. Stick to the basics: strong defense, ball control, good passes, shoot with power, aim small, miss small. Cougars on three. ONE, TWO, THREE…"

"COUGARS!"

Three minutes into the second half, the Cougars scored with a strong boot past the goalie, tying the game one to one. Both teams moved the ball aggressively up and down the field, but neither found the net. With only seconds remaining on the clock, a Jet headed a corner kick over Tripp's fingertips into the far corner. The game ended: Jets 2, Cougars 1.

"Good game, guys," Coach Tom told the team. "You played hard down to the last wire. I couldn't ask for a better effort. We'll get 'em next time. See you at practice on Tuesday. Cougars on three. ONE, TWO, THREE…"

"COUGARS!!"

"Hey, Jacob, wait up," Noah called as the team left the field.

"Yeah?" Jacob said.

"I…uh…I just wanted to say thanks for last night." Noah said.

"Man, I didn't know you were coming with Dustin. Promise." Jacob said.

"Well, thanks anyway. I made a dumb decision, and you did the right thing," Noah said.

"No, big deal," Jacob said. "Hey, why don't you ask Dustin to come to core group? I invited him. Maybe he'll come if you ask him, too."

"Dustin? To core group?"

"Sure, why not?" Jacob raised a hand and in a deep, Reverend-Wheeler-like voice boomed, "Let us go out to the highways and hedges, streets and country roads, and compel them to come, that God's house may be filled!"

The boys doubled over laughing.

"What's so funny?" Dustin called.

"Ah, nothing," Noah said. "Jacob's just being silly."

"Hey, this Wednesday is Halloween. You guys wanna trick or treat together?" Dustin asked.

"We're going to Trunk or Treat at the church; you could come with us," Noah said.

"What's Trunk or Treat?" Dustin asked.

"Everybody goes to the church parking lot and decorates their car trunks and hands out candy," Jacob explained.

Dustin laughed. "That's for babies."

"No, there's free food and really cool games and loads of candy. It's a blast," Noah said. "Coach Tom sets up half-court basketball every year. Will you come?"

Dustin shrugged. "Maybe."

~

The following Tuesday, Mark pedaled across campus to the School of Theology—a relatively new department of Indiana University approved in 1971. The genesis of religious studies at IU, however, dated back to 1910 when a local pastor began teaching non-credited Bible classes to students. In 1963, Supreme Court Justice Thomas Clark wrote: *"One's education is not complete without a study of comparative religion and its relationship to the advancement of civilization,"* thus fueling the religious-studies supporters' argument to establish an official School of Theology. In the school's first five years, enrollment jumped from 500 students to nearly 2,000.

In the lobby, Mark spoke to the receptionist. "Hello, I have an appointment with Dr. Denny at 10:00."

"Your name, please?" she asked.

"Mark...Mark Williams."

The young lady picked up a phone and pushed a button. "Mr. Williams is here to see you Dr. Denny...Yes, sir...Thank you. Dr. Denny says he'll see you now. Take the elevator to the second floor. His office is on the left, number 207."

"Thanks," Mark said.

Dr. Thomas Denny, professor of Old Testament and Hebrew, held Th.M. and Th.D. degrees from the New Orleans Theological Seminary and had done additional studies at Princeton and Oxford University. Though small in stature, the long-time professor stood tall in Biblical knowledge.

"Thank you, Dr. Denny, for meeting with me today," Mark said.

Dr. Denny shook Mark's hand and said, "How may I help you, Mr. Williams?"

Mark pulled the headstone rubbing from his backpack and handed it to the professor. "Can you tell me what these Hebrew characters mean?" he asked.

"Interesting," Dr. Denny mused. "Where did you copy the inscription?"

"From the headstone of one of the founding fathers of Hebron Community Church. It's on the cornerstone of the church building as well. Do you know what it means?"

Without hesitation, he answered, "Yes, the message reads: 'My brother's keeper.'"

REFLECTIONS

POINTS TO PONDER

Dr. Denny translated the Hebrew message to read: "my brother's keeper." What does this phrase mean to you?

_____

_____

WHAT DOES GOD SAY?

"Keep on loving each other as brothers and sisters." (Hebrews 13:1)

"What good is it, dear brothers and sisters, if you have faith but don't show it by your actions? Can that kind of faith save anyone? Suppose you see a brother or sister who has no food or clothing, and you say, 'Good-bye and have a good day; stay warm and eat well'—but then you don't give that person any food or clothing. What good does that do?" (James 2:14-16)

"And don't forget to do good and to share with those in need. These are the sacrifices that please God." (Hebrews 13:16)

LIVE WHAT YOU LEARN

This week, search for opportunities to help someone. Record your acts of kindness: _____

_____

_____

Chapter 18:
Trunk or Treat

Trunk or Treat opened at 5:30. The last gold and crimson leaves clung to tall trees. Twinkling stars dotted a clear sky over the churchyard, and dropping temperatures raced the setting sun.

Rebekah's teeth chattered. "Brr-willy! It's gettin' cold," she said.

Stephen, in full Captain Bellamy costume, snarled, "Aye, 'tis a bit chilly out here. Me thinks me patch has frozen to me eye. Aargh!"

Isaac giggled under a black, tricorne hat; Jacob and Elizabeth, also dressed as swashbucklers, looked at each other and rolled their eyes. On the pirate ship, a.k.a. the family mini-

131

van, bed-sheet sails snapped in the breeze and a homemade treasure chest overflowed with sweet treats.

Rebekah, sporting a gold-trimmed vest, black boots, and a sword, called, "Mateys, come to the Jolly Roger for your delectable, mouth-watering candies." She turned to Jacob, Elizabeth, and Isaac. "Kids, do you guys have your bags?"

"Yes, ma'am."

"Don't forget to report back to your dad or me every fifteen minutes or so. Go have fun!"

The kids galloped away to find friends. Elizabeth spotted Summer at the face-art booth and joined her in line.

"What are you gonna get?" she asked.

"I want the lioness face," Summer said. "What about you?"

Elizabeth studied the flamboyant designs. "Let me see. Oh, I like the butterfly. It's so colorful."

"Isaac, do you see any of your friends?" Jacob said.

"There's Elijah," he answered and darted off.

"I'm gonna go find Noah," Jacob called after him.

"Okay," Isaac yelled over his shoulder.

Rev. Wheeler and his wife, Sharon, parked their "farm" beside the Fickles' pirate ship. The couple wore matching, patched overalls and straw hats. Sharon emptied bags of Tootsie Roll Pops, Snickers, and Milky Ways into a wash tub.

She laughed. "Paul tried to hide the Milky Ways. They're his favorite."

Rebekah said, "Yeah, Stephen did the same thing with the Hershey dark chocolates."

A tap on the shoulder made Rebekah turn face to face with Pam Harper. *She must have come straight from work,* thought Rebekah, noting the charcoal business blazer and high heels.

"Pam! I'm so happy y'all came."

Kelly peaked from behind her mother's skirt.

Rebekah bowed to the little girl in pink taffeta and a sparkly tiara. "Princess Kelly, you look stunning, your royal highness."

Worry gripped Pam's mind like the steel-cast jaws of a bear trap and tears brimmed her dark-brown eyes. She asked nervously, "Have you seen Dustin?"

"Dustin? Uh, no, I haven't."

"He said he was coming to the church with Jacob and Noah, but with that boy, you just never… sometimes he…" Her voice trailed away.

"Stephen, will you man the ship, please? I'm going to help Pam look for Dustin," Rebekah said.

Stephen answered with a thumbs-up and an "aye-aye, matey." Rebekah linked elbows with Pam and reached for Kelly's hand. "This way, ladies. Isn't this fun? A lot of parents felt uncomfortable with Halloween, so our church started Trunk or Treat way back in the 90s to give families a safe alternative. Our kids love it. Have you ever been to Trunk or Treat, Kelly?"

Kelly shook her head.

"Well, you're gonna have a blast," Rebekah encouraged her.

"Hi, Rebekah. The pirate ship is adorable," a red-headed Raggedy Ann called from a nearby booth.

Rebekah smiled and waved. "Thanks, Holly. Love the costume! Like I was saying, our kids really look forward to this event every year, and Jacob's favorite part is right over here."

They rounded the last row of cars where tall, portable lights lit a concrete basketball court. Coach Tom, dressed as a referee, blew a whistle. A Jedi warrior passed the basketball to a pirate. The pirate dribbled under the hoop and passed to a giant roll of toilet paper—Dustin Harper.

Rebekah roared with laughter. "And there, Mrs. Harper," she sputtered between chortles, "is your boy. All safe and sound and exactly where he said he'd be."

Pam put her hand over her heart. "Thank goodness," she sighed.

"See, Mama," Kelly said. "I told you everything was okay."

"Kelly," Rebekah said and pointed to an SUV Cinderella castle, "see that pretty, blond piratess over there with a butterfly on her cheek? That's my daughter, Elizabeth, and her friend, Summer. Pam, do you mind if Kelly walks around with the girls?"

"Can I, Mama? Pleeease!" Kelly begged.

"I guess so," said Pam.

"Great!" Rebekah gave the little girl a high five. "Elizabeth!" she called and motioned, "come over here. I want you to meet Pam and Kelly."

Elizabeth and Summer came giggling and holding up swollen, goody bags. "Look, Mom," Elizabeth said. "We have a *ton* of candy."

"Well, don't *eat* a ton candy or you'll be sick," Rebekah warned. "Girls, this is Kelly, Dustin's little sister, and this is his mom, Mrs. Harper. Why don't you girls take Kelly around and show her the games and all the decorated cars."

Elizabeth reached for Kelly's hand. "Sure! Come on, Kelly." Summer took Kelly's other hand, and the three girls skipped toward the pick-up-ducks game.

"Don't let her out of your sight!" Rebekah called after them.

"We won't," Elizabeth hollered back.

"Let's go get some hot chocolate," Rebekah said. "I'm freezing."

A stout man dressed as Fred Flintstone poured two cups of steaming cocoa. "Marshmallows, ladies?"

"Yabba dabba doo!" Rebekah said with a grin. "Thanks, Jack. Jack Penny, meet my new friend, Pam Harper."

"Nice to meet you, Pam."

"You, too, Jack."

Rebekah pointed to an empty picnic table. "Let's sit over there," she said and waved to Snow White. "Hi, Mary Lou."

"Do you know everybody here?" Pam marveled.

"Not everyone, but most. Stephen and I moved from Alabama to Clear Creek fourteen years ago, and the first thing we did was search for a church home. We found Hebron Community Church, and it's been our family away from family ever since. We love it here. And now Stephen's the children's director."

"That's nice."

"Being part of a community of believers has been *so* good for our family—good for our marriage, good for the kids. Pam, I really hope you and Dustin and Kelly will come check it out sometime soon."

Pam sipped the hot chocolate. "This is delicious," she said.

"Do you have family nearby?" Rebekah asked.

"No, not really. My parents divorced when I was a teenager. My dad lives in Florida now. We don't talk much, and mom...well, she died five years ago."

"I'm so sorry, Pam. That must be really hard for you, especially with your husband...uh, away."

"You have no idea," Pam said. Tears refilled her eyes.

"May I pray for you?" Rebekah asked.

"Sure."

Rebekah took Pam's hands in hers.

"What?" Pam said. "You mean right now? Here?"

"No better time to talk to God than the present."

"Uh…okay."

Rebekah closed her eyes. "Lord Jesus, thank You so much for dying on the cross in our place and opening the way for us to come to God's throne of grace as often as we will. Thank You for our new friends, Pam and Dustin and Kelly. Lord, please help them understand how much You love them and how much we care. Please help Pam in all the difficult things that are set before her— raising Dustin and Kelly alone, paying the bills, looking after their home. Help her every day, Lord. Please give her strength and peace and hope as only You can. And, Lord, I don't know Mr. Harper's circumstances, but please bless him and keep him safe and help him know that You're with him and for him. Please make a way for this family to be reunited and please redeem all that has been damaged and lost. In Jesus' name I pray, Amen," she prayed and then opened her eyes to Pam's tear-streaked face.

Pam's voice quavered. "Thank you, Rebekah."

Rebekah hugged her tightly and said, "Hold on to Jesus, Pam. Every day, hold onto Him."

"Bill," she whispered.

"What?"

"Bill. My husband's name is William Harper. Everyone calls him Bill."

Pam scanned the crowd. Toddlers on dads' shoulders. Moms cleaning cotton candy from sticky fingers. Everyone seemed so happy. *We were a happy family once upon a time,* she thought. *Twenty-eight long months since Bill's arrest for misappropriating those bank funds; it feels like twenty-eight years!*

~

"Embezzlement" the charges read—a Class 1 Felony. With the guilty verdict came a $1000 fine and a three-year prison sentence.

"How could you do this, Bill? How could you do this to our family?" Pam had asked in heartbroken bewilderment.

Bill choked. "I never intended for it to go this far. I promise. We had all those medical bills from your surgery—not that I'm blaming you. I knew it was wrong, but I just thought I could borrow enough to catch up on things and then pay it back before anyone noticed. It was stupid; I know. I'm so sorry, Pam. I'm so, so sorry."

~

Rebekah glanced at her watch and pulled Pam's arm. "Come on," she said. "You don't wanna miss this. It's Stephen's turn in the dunking booth."

Pam gawked. "Dunking booth? On a freezing night like tonight?"

"Yep, all the money goes toward the youth mission trip. Oh, the things we'll do for Jesus and our kids!" she said with a laugh.

REFLECTIONS

POINTS TO PONDER

Bill Harper knew what he did was wrong, but he thought he could fix it before anyone _____ out.

WHAT DOES GOD SAY

"For all that is secret will eventually be brought into the open, and everything that is concealed will be brought to light and made known by all." (Luke 8:17)

"People who conceal their sins will not prosper, but if they confess and turn from them, they will receive mercy." (Proverbs 28:13)

"The night is almost gone; the day of salvation will soon be here. So, remove your dark deeds like dirty clothes, and put on the shining armor of right living." (Romans 13:12)

LIVE WHAT YOU LEARN

God knows every "secret" sin, but there's good news. He promises that if we confess our sins to Him, He will faithfully forgive us (1 John 1:9) and help us do what is right. Do you have a "secret" sin? Confess to Jesus now and receive His forgiveness.

CHAPTER 19:
EUREKA!

At core group on Friday, Mark taught the boys the value of eternal prayers. "As we study the prayers of Paul, notice that he rarely asked God to meet temporal or temporary needs. He constantly prayed for the eternal things of God. Open your Bibles to Ephesians chapter 1. Noah, will you read verses fifteen through twenty for us? And by the way, Dustin, we're really glad you joined us today."

Noah read, "Ever since I first heard of your strong faith in the Lord Jesus Christ and your love for God's people everywhere, I have not stopped thanking God for you. I pray for you constantly, asking God, the glorious Father of our Lord Jesus Christ, to give you a spiritual wisdom and insight so that your hearts will be flooded with light so that you can understand the confident hope He has given to those He called—His holy people who are His rich and glorious inheritance. I also pray that you will understand the incredible greatness of God's power for us who believe in Him. This is the same mighty power that raised Christ from the dead and seated Him in the place of honor at God's right hand in the heavenly realms."

"Did Paul ask for good health?" said Mark.

"No," the boys answered.

"Paul wrote Ephesians from prison. Did he ask God to get him out of jail?"

Dustin's eyes fell to the floor.

"Nope."

"Then what did he pray for?" Mark asked.

"He asked God to give the people wisdom and insight," Charlie said.

Jacob groaned. "I need wisdom and insight. Mrs. Culpepper's research paper is due two weeks from today, and I still don't know what Mission-T is."

Mark nodded. "And I still don't have the answer to Professor Sparrow's riddle. Why don't we stop right now and ask God for His wisdom? Jacob, will you pray?"

"Sure." Jacob bowed his head. "Dear Lord, thank You for this day and thank You for another opportunity to study Your word. Lord, please give us wisdom and insight to understand the riddle…"

From seemingly nowhere, a phrase from the riddle flashed into Mark's mind: The truth that hides.

143

Mark thought, *Hides...Professor Sparrow said to think deeper, and the journal said there was a large stockade of medical supplies, food, and water.*

Jacob continued praying, "And figure out what Mission-T is. In Jesus' name I pray. Amen."

Mark shouted, "Amen! Hey, guys, it just hit me. There's got to be some sort of hidden room or something—maybe even a cellar!"

"Why?" Jacob asked.

"The clues. Asa Watts wrote in his journal that the men worked nonstop for three years and collected a stockade of medical supplies and food. Where would they have stored all that stuff in this tiny church? Professor Sparrow told me to 'think *deeper*.' Maybe there's a hidden cellar or a room connected to the church. Come on guys. Search the walls. The floor. Everywhere!"

The boys jumped from their seats and scoured every corner of Fellowship Hall.

Every nook.

Every cranny.

"I'll check the stairs," Noah said.

Nothing.

With hands on his hips, Mark paced back and forth, back and forth in front of the solid-oak altar sitting against the back wall of fellowship hall. A white-linen cloth with three golden-thread, embroidered crosses and coordinating gold, chainette fringe covered the carved cabinet. A pair of golden candlesticks and a large Bible opened to the Gospel of John, chapter three rested on top.

"There's got to be something—somewhere," Mark said.

"Or maybe Professor Sparrow just sent you on a wild goose chase." Dustin laughed and leaned his full weight against the heavy table. It scooted backwards.

"Careful, Dustin," Jacob said. "The altar's kinda sacred. You really shouldn't lean on it."

"Oh, sorry," Dustin said. He strained to pull it back into place but stopped abruptly.

"Hey, Jacob, look!" He pointed to a narrow strip of wood flush with the concrete floor now visible from under the altar.

Jacob dropped to his knees. "Mark!" he shouted. "Look what Dustin found!"

The group swarmed to Dustin and Jacob like bugs to a porch light.

Dustin cried, "Come on, guys. Let's move this altar-thingy."

"No! Wait," Mark yelled. "We need to ask Rev. Wheeler first."

"I'll get him," Jacob volunteered. He sprinted up the steps and barely knocked before bursting into the pastor's office.

"Well, come in, Jacob," Rev. Wheeler said.

"Rev. Wheeler, you gotta come see this. We prayed for wisdom and insight, and then all the clues just started coming together in Mark's head that there might be a hidden cellar or something, and then Dustin leaned on the altar, and it scooted backwards, and we found a board, and we think it might be a trap door to a secret room!"

Rev. Wheeler laughed. "Calm down, Jacob. I'm coming."

Jacob and the pastor hurried downstairs where Mark showed Rev. Wheeler Dustin's discovery. "Is it okay to move the altar?" he asked.

Rev. Wheeler grinned and wedged in behind the table. "Come on, boys. Let's push this thing toward the middle of the room."

"Move the chairs out of the way, guys. Then everyone come back here," Mark said eagerly.

With folding chairs cleared, Rev. Wheeler, Mark, and eleven seventh-graders placed their hands on the heavy table. "Ready? on three. One, two, three, PUSH!" Mark shouted.

The altar scraped a few inches across the floor. "Again," Mark called, "one, two, three, PUSH!"

A hinge appeared.

"One more time," Rev. Wheeler said.

Mark shouted, "One, two, three, PUSH!"

This time, the altar lurched forward uncovering a rough trap door with a hand-cut pull hole.

"Rev. Wheeler, will you do the honors?" Mark said breathlessly.

The old hinges creaked in protest as the pastor raised the trap door hiding a deep, black hole. Mark threw both hands into the air.

"Eureka!" he cried.

REFLECTIONS

POINTS TO PONDER

When they discovered the hidden, underground room, Mark shouted, "Eureka!" meaning a cry of joy when one finds or discovers something. We cheer wildly for football or basketball or baseball or soccer teams, but who does the Bible say should evoke our shouts of joy? The

---

WHAT DOES GOD SAY?

"Shout with joy to the LORD, all the earth! Worship the LORD with gladness. Come before Him, singing with joy!" (Psalm 100:1-2)

"Come, let us sing to the LORD! Let us shout joyfully to the Rock of our salvation. Let us come to Him with thanksgiving. Let us sing psalms of praise to Him. For the LORD is a great God, a great King above all gods." (Psalm 95:1-3)

"Come, everyone! Clap your hands! Shout to God with joyful praise! For the LORD Most High is awesome. He is the great King of all the earth." (Psalm 47:1-2)

LIVE WHAT WE LEARN

Jesus is worthy of your worship and praise and thanksgiving! Determine to give God more handclaps and shouts of praise than anything else in your life.

CHAPTER 20:
MISSION-T

"We need a flashlight," Rev. Wheeler said.

"I've got one in the pack on my bike. Be right back." Mark said.

"Careful, boys, don't fall in," Rev. Wheeler cautioned.

Mark shot up the stairs like greased lightning and returned in seconds. He shined the ultra-bright beam from an LED-tactical flashlight into the dark hole. A frayed, rope ladder dangled from the opening to the ground.

"I'll go down," Dustin volunteered.

Rev. Wheeler held out his arm to block the way. "Wait, son. Those ropes are old and rotten; we need a ladder."

The pastor handed his cell phone to Jacob. "Jacob, call your dad and ask him to please come to the church with a ladder and additional flashlights."

Jacob's fingers trembled as he punched the buttons.

149

"Hello," Stephen said.

Jacob spouted, "Dad, Rev. Wheeler needs you to bring a ladder and flashlights to the basement at church."

"When?" his dad said.

"Right now, and hurry!"

"Is someone hurt?" Stephen asked with concern.

"No, sir. Nobody's hurt. I'll explain when you get here."

"On my way, Bud."

"Okay, thanks, Dad. Bye." Jacob hung up. "He's coming."

In minutes, Stephen walked down the steps with a long ladder over one shoulder. He found the boys and Mark and Rev. Wheeler on hands and knees peering into a deep hole.

"What in the world?" he exclaimed.

"It's a hidden room, Dad!" Jacob said excitedly.

Stephen extended the twelve-foot ladder and eased it into the hole. "Mark, hold the ladder; I'll go down."

"Can I go, too?" Jacob begged.

"No, Bud. Let me see what's down there first."

Mark and Rev. Wheeler held the ladder steady. Stephen climbed down and stepped cautiously onto a hard-packed, dirt floor. The air felt cool and damp, and a musty odor filled his nostrils. He shined the light in all directions and discovered a small room where two timber-framed tunnels intersected—one running due west and the other southwest.

"It's like a coal mine," Stephen shouted from below, his voice echoing into the darkness. "There are two passageways. I'm gonna walk down the west wing to see where it goes."

"Be careful, Stephen," Rev. Wheeler cautioned.

The brilliant beam illuminated a footpath and barren walls abandoned for decades—a world left unto itself. Stephen ran his hand over the decaying wood and stepped deeper into the tunnel.

Five minutes passed.

No one spoke in Fellowship Hall.

Ten minutes.

Mark tapped his foot nervously.

Rev. Wheeler shouted, "Stephen, can you hear me?"

No answer.

Tick, tick, tick.

Every minute seemed like an hour.

"Coming up," Stephen finally called. At the top of the ladder, he cried, "This place is unbelievable! Those tunnels seem to run on for miles."

"I wonder where they go?" Mark said.

"So, this underground system has to be the Mission-T that Asa Watts wrote about," Rev. Wheeler said. "Mission: *Tunnels*. I can't wait to tell Miss Alice. Boys, you're all part of a remarkable, historical discovery!"

Hoots, back slaps, and high fives bounced around the basement.

"It all makes sense now," Mark said. "*From times gone by a mystery lies*—underground. And the *secret to unveil* is this hidden tunnel system running under Clear Creek where the brave and courageous saints of Hebron Community Church fed and cared for hungry and hurting people throughout the Civil War—northerners and southerners, black and white, rich and poor, young and old—*the story never told*."

Jacob jumped up and down, pumping his fists in the air. He shouted at the top of his lungs. "We finally solved the history mystery!!!"

Mark pointed heavenward. "Thank You, Lord Jesus!" he cried. "Thank You, thank You, thank You!"

~

At midnight, Professor Sparrow opened his email and discovered a message from MWilliams@theUniversity.edu. He clicked and read:

"From times gone by

A mystery lies,

A secret to unveil.

The truth that hides

From modern eyes

Are tunnels dug large-scale.

And ones so brave

And bold those days

Could not be called the sleepers,

They chose the right

For black and white

To be their brothers' keepers."

Professor Sparrow's jaw dropped. "Well, old boy, he did it."

"Meow."

"Mark Williams really did it. He unraveled the riddle. Our forty-year-old mystery has been solved…at last." The professor threw back his head and laughed.

And laughed.

And laughed until salty tears filled craggy cheeks. He hit reply and typed:

Mr. Williams,

I request the honor of your presence at my home this Sunday afternoon, November 4th, at 3:00 o'clock sharp, and please bring young Mr. Fickle with you.

Respectfully yours,

Prof. Benjamin H. Sparrow

REFLECTIONS
POINTS TO PONDER

God helped Mark and Jacob solve Professor Sparrow's riddle and unveil the Civil War history mystery. Do you know that God reveals a mind-boggling mystery in the Bible's New Testament?   YES   NO

WHAT DOES GOD SAY?

"God Himself revealed His mysterious plan...God did not reveal it to previous generations, but now by His Spirit He has revealed it to His holy apostles and prophets. And this is God's plan: both Gentiles and Jews who believe the Good News share equally in the riches inherited by God's children. Both are part of the same body and enjoy the promise of blessings because they belong to Christ Jesus." (Ephesians 3:3-6)

"This message was kept secret for centuries and generations past, but now it has been revealed to God's people...And this is the secret: Christ lives in you...So we tell others about Christ." (Colossians 1:26-28)

LIVE WHAT YOU LEARN

This is God's mystery: Christ lives in those who believe the Good News of forgiveness and eternal life through Jesus—a FREE gift from God. This week tell someone God's Good-News mystery.

CHAPTER 21:
REWIND

The following cold, Sunday afternoon, the college freshman and seventh grader marched up Professor Sparrow's front steps. Two neglected rockers and a porch swing furnished the otherwise bare veranda. Mark rang the doorbell and winked at a very nervous Jacob. The boy's stomach churned like the gray clouds overhead.

"The weatherman says we might get our first big snow tonight," Mark commented in an effort to calm his young friend.

Jacob tried to smile, but his dry-as-a-cotton-bowl lips smacked together instead. Mark grinned and slapped him on the back. Slow footsteps approached; the heavy door opened wide.

"Mr. Williams," Professor Sparrow said and shook Mark's hand. "And this must be Jacob Fickle. Please, come in, gentlemen."

"Thank you, sir. Go ahead, Jacob," Mark said.

The boys followed Professor Sparrow into the library. Jacob eyed the book-lined walls. He thought, *Professor Sparrow must have more books than my whole school.*

The old man hobbled behind the mahogany desk and motioned to two, wooden armchairs with curved backs and threadbare, needlepoint seats. As soon as Mark and Jacob sat down, Morton curled around Jacob's blue jeans. The boy ran a hand along the arched back.

"Mr. Williams, I believe congratulations are in order," Professor Sparrow began. "I'd be most interested to hear how you cracked the riddle and found the tunnels."

"Well, sir, I thought I'd never figure it out when you told me that the Underground Railroad was the wrong answer, but I still had a strong hunch that the mystery was tied to the Civil War."

"On what basis?" the professor asked.

"The words from the Battle Hymn of the Republic."

Professor Sparrow nodded.

Mark put a hand on Jacob's shoulder. "And Jacob here was a big help. He's part of my core group at Hebron Community Church. Since he's working on a history paper about Clear Creek, we decided to collaborate our efforts and work together. One Friday, after our meeting, we found the church's Statement of Faith and learned that just like the city of Hebron remained a Levitical refuge in the Kingdom of Israel, the church had pledged back in the 1800s to remain a refuge—a *safe house*—for men, women, and children of every kindred, tongue, people, and nation. That's when the idea came to mind that the *her* in the riddle might be the church—our church—and we set up a meeting with Rev. Wheeler."

"Yes, I've met Paul Wheeler. Good man," Professor Sparrow said.

"Well, as it turned out, he couldn't answer our questions, but he introduced us to Miss Alice—uh, Mrs. Alice Holtshausen—the church historian."

The professor nodded again. "And you learned that I own Asa Watts' house, her great-great-grandfather and a founding father of Hebron Community Church."

"Yes, sir. And Miss Alice shared parts of his old journal where he wrote about Mission–T. We learned that it took three years to complete and that it was well stocked with supplies and water, but we couldn't figure out what or where Mission-T actually was until we put two and two together. One, the church building would have been too tiny to hold a mountain of supplies; plus, two, you told me to 'think deeper.' So, we searched for a hidden room or underground cellar."

"And my friend, Dustin, accidently moved the altar in the basement and uncovered a trap door," Jacob chimed in. "And that's how we found the tunnels."

Professor Sparrow applauded. "Well done, men. Well done."

"Professor Sparrow, now that you've heard our story, we're very eager to hear *you*rs. How did you find those tunnels forty years ago? And why did you keep them a secret all this time?" Mark asked.

The professor leaned back in his chair. His elbows propped on the cracked-leather arms; fingertips drummed together. A heavy silence draped the worn library, and a faraway look settled over the aged face. Professor Sparrow rewound the hands of time.

"I've always been intrigued with American history—even at your age, Jacob," he started. "I pursued that love with an American history major at Princeton and then moved on to grad school at the University of Chicago. After earning my doctorate, I landed an associate professorship here at IU. When I started house hunting in Clear Creek, Mrs. Holtshausen had just put the old Watts home on the market, and I couldn't resist it. It was like moving into a history museum. The first weeks after I moved in, I searched every inch of this old house looking for historical artifacts, and eventually, I found this in the attic."

He pulled a rusted, metal chest from the bottom drawer and set it on the desk. Using a skeleton key from his coat pocket, the professor unlocked the box and carefully spread out before the eager boys a yellowed map and a handwritten paper entitled Mission-T. Mark and Jacob perched on the edge of their seats as Professor Sparrow showed them the detailed diagram of a triangular-shaped tunnel system connecting the cellar of the Asa Watts' house to the basements of Hebron Community Church and the university's history building.

Professor Sparrow's eyes twinkled. "These documents I unearthed were mind-boggling. Look." On the map, he pointed out a hidden staircase tucked behind classroom #507 of the history building that descended into the underground tunnel.

"So that's how you vanished so fast that day," Mark said.

He chuckled. "Yes, that day and numerous times before—a mind-blowing phenomenon for my students over the years, I must say. After finding the secret staircase and Mission-T, I spent days exploring the long-abandoned passageways that validate the never-told story of the courageous men and women of 19th century Clear Creek, Indiana."

"Why didn't you tell somebody?" Jacob asked.

"I never intended to keep such an important discovery to myself. Truly, I didn't. But I was young and adventurous and considered it amusing to give my students that first semester the challenge of solving a baffling, historical riddle. But the problem was, they never unraveled the puzzle, nor did my students the following semester, nor the semester after that. Then semesters rolled into years. I became so entangled in the web of secrecy that my very life became a secret—much like those clandestine tunnels. I withdrew from the world like a turtle in its dark, lonely shell. And, sadly to say, I hid there for forty, long years."

The professor looked down and shook his head.

"Professor Sparrow," Mark said gently, "a wise man once said to focus on one thing: forgetting the past and looking forward to what lies ahead."

The professor offered a half-smile. "The Apostle Paul," he murmured. "Philippians chapter three, verse thirteen."

Mark marveled at the professor's biblical knowledge. "Yes, sir, that's right. And today, I believe the turtle has come out of that lonely shell and found two new friends eagerly wanting to get to know him better."

The wrinkled eyes welled with tears. "Thank you, Mark. Thank you, Jacob. Thank you, both."

REFLECTIONS

POINTS TO PONDER

Prof. Sparrow became so tangled in the web of secrecy that he _____ from other people.

WHAT DOES GOD SAY?

"Then the LORD God said, 'It is not good for man to be alone...'" (Genesis 2:18)

"Two people are better than one, for they can help each other succeed. If one person falls, the other can reach out and help. But someone who falls alone is in real trouble." (Ecclesiastes 4:9-10)

"Let us think of ways to motivate one another to acts of love and good works. And let us not neglect our meeting together, as some people do, but encourage one another, especially now that the day of Christ's return is drawing near." (Hebrews 10:24-25)

LIVE WHAT YOU LEARN

Make a list of three people you will encourage this week and do it. Remember, God designed us to live life together. Never isolate yourself, dear one. It's a lonely and dangerous place to hide!

CHAPTER 22:
LIVE WHAT YOU LEARN

Jacob Fickle

Mrs. Culpepper

Seventh-grade English

November 16, 2018

The Civil War History Mystery of Clear Creek, Indiana

Clear Creek is a small town in Perry Township, Monroe County, in the U.S. state of Indiana and was named after a local creek. The Clear Creek stream is a tributary of Salt Creek, which flows into the East Fork of Indiana's White River.

According to the 2010 census, Clear Creek's population is 5,000. It has three schools: Clear Creek Elementary, Clear Creek Middle (where I am a student), and Clear Creek High School and four churches—the oldest one is Hebron Community Church.

The Church Charter for Hebron Community Church was signed on April 3, 1829, and the building's cornerstone or keystone was set by masons on April 21st of that same year. In the church Statement of Faith, the founding fathers resolved, and I quote, *"As the city of Hebron remained a Levitical refuge in the Kingdom of Israel, so shall Hebron Community Church forever remain a refuge in the great state of Indiana—a safe house for men, women, and children of every kindred, and tongue and people, and nation. So, help us God."* In keeping with the Statement of Faith, the church cornerstone and later the headstones of the first pastor and founding fathers were engraved with the following Hebrew characters: שומר אחי

Dr. Thomas Denny of Indiana University's School of Theology translated the inscription. The Hebrew phrase means: "My Brother's Keeper."

One of the church founding fathers, Asa Hartford Watts, left a journal that is now owned by his great-great-granddaughter, Mrs. Alice Murphey Holtshausen. An entry in the old journal dated Sunday, July 4, 1858, reported that as war between the northern and southern states threatened the nation, Rev. Jeremiah Walvoord and his elders initiated what they called Mission-T. Watts' journal does not disclose the nature of the secret mission.

In 1978, however, Prof. Benjamin H. Sparrow, a history professor at Indiana University, discovered a locked, metal box in the attic of Asa Watts' house (now owned by Prof. Sparrow). The box contained a comprehensive description of the project and a detailed map of an underground tunnel system that runs from a hidden stairwell in the history building at IU to the cellar of the Watts house (4,657 feet), from the cellar of the Watts house to the basement of Hebron Community Church (2,489 feet), and from Hebron Community Church back to the history building (5,280 feet), forming a scalene triangle. (See diagram A.)

The tunnel triangle was hand dug with picks and shovels by men working day and night from Hebron Community Church and many humanitarian sympathizers from the university. It took three years to complete the tunnels and stock them with medical supplies, food, and water.

The Civil War officially began at 4:30 a.m. on April 12, 1861 when Confederate cannons opened fire on Fort Sumter. According to the Corydon Battle Park website, only one Civil War battle was fought on Indiana soil. The battle *"occurred on July 9, 1863 when 450 members of the Harrison County Home Guard attempted to delay General John Hurt Morgan's 2,400 Confederate soldiers that day, in hopes that the Union reinforcements would arrive and stop Morgan's march through southern Indiana. Indiana Governor at the time, Oliver P. Morton, on receiving news of the invasion, issued a proclamation ordering all able-bodied male citizens in the counties south of the National Road to form into companies and to arm themselves with such arms they could procure. In a short but spirited battle, lasting less than an hour, Morgan met his first and only organized resistance in the Hoosier State. By outflanking both wings at the same time, Morgan's men completely routed the militia. Four guards were killed, several were wounded, 355 were captured, and the remainder escaped. The victory was not without cost to the Raiders. Eleven Raiders were killed and forty wounded."*

The secret, underground tunnels of Clear Creek along with IU's history building, Hebron Community Church, and Asa Watts' house served as shelters and a hospital throughout the Civil War for hungry, hurting, and wounded people regardless of their race, gender, or economic status. Asa Watts recorded that both Union and Confederate soldiers and sympathizers were served at Mission-T.

Across his forty years of teaching at Indiana University, Prof. Sparrow frequently used the hidden stairwell behind his classroom to access the tunnel. He regularly walked the passageway between the history building and the old Watts house. For safety purposes, however, the tunnels are now closed to the public, and a team of archeologists from IU are studying the underground passageways and the artifacts found in them. So far, they have uncovered weapons, tools, glass bottles, leather boots, and tin cups dating back to the 1800s.

In November 1861, Julia Ward Howe wrote the Battle Hymn of the Republic six months after those first mortars hit Fort Sumter. The last stanza reads: *"In the beauty of the lilies Christ was born across the sea, with a glory in His bosom that transfigures you and me. As He died to make men holy, let us live to make men free, while God is marching on.* Like Mrs. Howe's well-known hymn, the bold and brave members of Hebron Community Church lived and died for people of every kindred, tongue, people, and nation and courageously upheld the United States Declaration of Independence, which proclaims: *"We hold these truths to be self-evident, that all men are created equal, that they are endowed by their Creator with certain unalienable Rights, that among these are Life, Liberty, and the Pursuit of Happiness."*

In conclusion, writing this research paper was at first, and I quote: *"a pain in the derriere."* This assignment, however, has taught me the value of putting others before myself and the truth that all people are created equal. I pray that I will follow my church core group's motto and *live what I have learned.* So, help me God.

Diagram A:

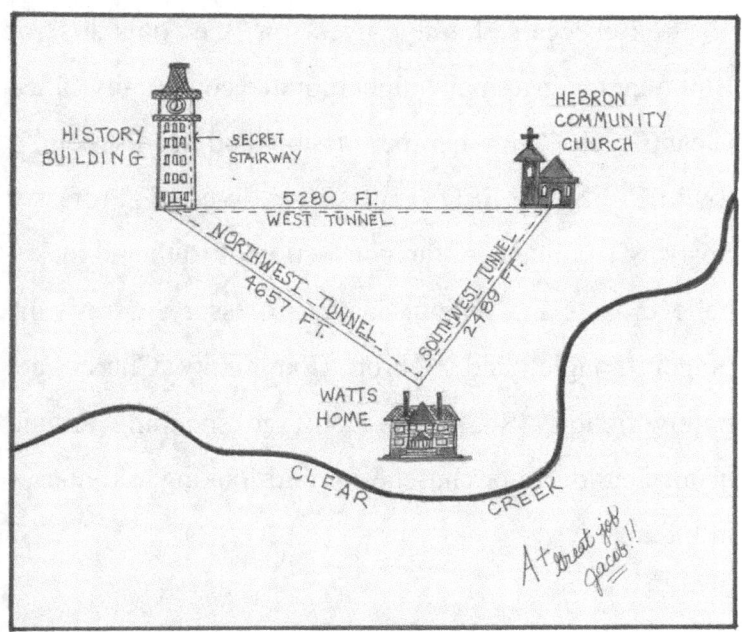

AFTERWORD

When our three Indiana grandkids were little tikes, their mother (our daughter, Rebecca) made up a story about a fictitious Professor Sparrow that lives in an intriguing, for-real house in Bloomington, Indiana. Although they've never met the true owners, in her story, a tunnel runs from the professor's house to Indiana University, and he put spiders in Halloween candy. In Rebecca's rendition, there's also a portal in the old mansion that transports Professor Sparrow to their neighbors' attic. ☺

Rebecca's family lives on the outskirts of Bloomington in a small unincorporated community called Clear Creek. With her permission and God's help, I joyfully ENLARGED and s-t-r-e-t-c-h-e-d Professor Sparrow's tall tale—a fun concoction of truth and make-believe, facts and fiction. Sadly, Professor Sparrow, the tunnel triangle, and Hebron Community Church are purely fiction. (So, please don't go snooping around history buildings or churches or odd-looking, old houses in Indiana.)

Beloved, I hope you enjoyed *Professor Sparrow and the Clear Creek History Mystery*. May we all learn to put others before ourselves, respect that all people are created and equally loved by God regardless of race, gender, or economic status, and strive to live what we have learned. So, help us God!

Jill

Illustrator: ANYA FIGERT, a sixth grader at Clear Creek Christian School, loves animals, drawing, Irish step-dancing, and running barefoot through the grass. She lives in Bloomington, Indiana with her parents, Stephen and Rebecca, two brothers, Easton and Fisher, and beloved pets, Lucy, Summer, Squirt, and Shiloh. Anya is an active member of Sherwood Oaks Christian Church, where her dad serves as children's ministry director.

Cover Art: FORREST WALKER is an artist and visual designer raised in the South and trained in San Francisco at the Academy of Art University. Forrest specializes in digital illustration for book covers and conceptual art as well as branding identity projects and finds his inspiration in classic American illustration, comic books, and film conceptual art.